A BLOCK FROM MY HOTEL, THE GODS DESCENDED

We have three Gods. Three unknown and terrible Gods.

They live Up-Top: perigee 21,180 miles, apogee 22,652 miles. Nothing on Earth is beyond their reach.

They can pull down buildings, walk un-inhibited through walls of brick and steel. They're invisible when they wish to be, wrathful when their wish is thwarted. Right now they were hunting me. Gil Warren—the most wanted man on Earth.

A block from my hotel, the Gods descended, in swirling snow and surging wind. A man on the other side of the street began to climb eerily into the sky. His feet thrashed, his face revealed shock.

As far as I could see, the man's only crime was to have dark hair and my approximate build. He twisted futilely in an invisible massive grip, his frightened cries muted by the wind.

Letting out a long breath, I turned left at the first corner I came to. The incident had occurred too close to my hotel to be a coincidence; I couldn't go back there.

THE BABYLON GATE

EDWARD A. BYERS

BAEN
SCIENCE FICTION
BOOKS

Acknowledgments:
Jim Baen and Bob Sabella.

THE BABYLON GATE

A Baen Books Original

Baen Publishing Enterprises
260 Fifth Avenue
New York, N.Y. 10001

First printing, April 1986

ISBN: 0-671-65565-5

Cover art by Bob Eggleton

Printed in the United States of America

Distributed by
SIMON & SCHUSTER
TRADE PUBLISHING GROUP
1230 Avenue of the Americas
New York, N.Y. 10020

This book is for Lola

Prologue

Pete Stillus, Navigator First Class, poked his head and shoulders out of the belly turret, tapped me once on the knee to get my attention, then glanced around at the other two dockrats.

"We got us a war," he said. His face was drawn, ashen.

"Come on, Pete," Lieutenant Jim Barnes muttered in an aggrieved tone. "There's a truce in effect, remember?"

Pete just shrugged, his round face tense.

There were three cameras located on top of the Observation and Control vehicle, two more on each side. I was responsible for getting film of all enemy action. I swung the left side cameras around, took a look at dusty brown African landscape. I angled the cameras up by ten degrees. *Oh, boy!* Less than a dozen kilometers away, I caught a glimpse of something metallic.

"Tanks," I said.

"You're welcome," Pete murmured, lips twisting into a sick grin. He shot his eyes heavenward and disappeared into his hole like a reverse jack-in-the-box.

To my right Lieutenant Barnes and Signalman Alex

Metcalf became suddenly animated. They began punching numbers into the console computer. A topographical map popped up on one of the CRTs, grid lines overlaying it. Everyone inside Obscon-27 was suddenly very busy.

"When are we going to start *moving*?" Alex asked, as though any of us could tell him. He looked apprehensively at a series of dots that had appeared on the screen. The dots—hundreds of them—were moving inexorably toward us.

Above us, in geosynchronous orbit, the Fannon VI War Computer was probably scratching its head. The dots, as I could now see on the side and top screens, were ordinary infantry, backed up by mechanized assault units.

I suppose I should have felt comforted that Fanny VI was a hundred times smarter than anything the opposition had, able to run through a billion permutations in the time it took to blink an eye. The problem was something else. Fanny VI didn't give a tinker's dam about whether we dockrats—for (D)eployed (O)bservational (C)ontrol—survived the battle. Personnel in the field were inconsequential. Fanny VI was interested only in *grand strategy*, i.e., the final outcome.

The enemy moved toward us, unhindered, for most of an hour. Time inside the observation vehicle seemed to slow down by a factor of five.

"They've stopped," Alex said then, relieved. He pointed to the screen with a skinny finger. The dots had halted their advance and even retreated a little. On the audios I could hear the *cr-rump* sound mortar fire makes. There was a lot of it.

"O-*kay*!" Pete exclaimed in relief. He poked his head up out of the well, gave us all a sunny smile.

"Fanny's decided to keep them busy," Lieutenant Barnes said phlegmatically. "We can relax a bit." So saying, he put his hands behind his head and leaned back as far as his harness would allow. He appeared to fall asleep.

We weren't supposed to really *be* in a battle. The Western Bloc and Eastern Bloc seldom allowed a real exchange of gunfire. They just moved us chess pieces around on the board until one side or the other yelled "uncle." I took one more look and put the cameras on automatic. Then I popped the vehicle's top hatch, crawled up the three-step ladder, and emerged into bright February sunshine. It felt good on my neck and arms. Alex crawled up beside me, seating himself on the cowling.

To the right and left of the Observation vehicle were the twenty units that made up SubCom-27. They were all motionless now, armor-plated copters the size of railroad cars. A command from Fanny VI would send them exploding into action. Each subcom could move with dizzying speed, and possessed enough firepower to level a fair-sized city. There were sixty subcoms in this particular fracas.

"What do you think happened to the truce?" Alex asked.

I glanced at Alex, who was about as unlikely a person for observation duty as I'd seen. Given that dockrats were a special breed, Alex was in a class all by himself. Tall—six feet six inches—and lath thin, he was like a giant spider inside the observation vehicle.

I said, "What *always* happens to the truce? This war's been going on for how long . . . three years?" I gave a shrug. "Gives both sides a chance to try out new weapons. Maybe neither of them *wants* to stop it."

"What about the African countries? They want it stopped."

"Fat chance of that. They have the natural resources the Eastern Bloc needs. Some of them made the mistake of inviting the spider in."

"And we're seeing the spider doesn't take too big a bite."

"Looks like."

Alex put both hands on the edge of the cowling and scanned the grassy landscape. This part of Niger, south of the mountains, was mostly savannas. Here and there, though, were a few rocky escarpments, isolated monoliths.

"You're a cynic, Gil, you know that? That's the trouble with you." He shook his head, then removed a hand from the cowling and used it to scratch his nose. Grinning, he said, "I guess it comes of getting too much education. Me, I'm happy the way I am. Another two tours and I'll get out, maybe buy me a little fishing boat down on the Gulf of Mexico."

I happened to know that he had a degree in engineering, but I let it go. Before becoming a dockrat I'd spent four years chasing a doctorate in languages. I was *still* chasing it—lacking only the dissertation—a fact that amused my fellow rats no end.

There was a series of thunderclaps in the direction of the enemy.

"Fanny's slapping a few wrists."

"Maybe they'll finally see reason," I said. "There's not an army in the world that can stand up to Fanny."

Alex stretched mightily, then pulled his arms down and squinted at the patches of smoke that were drifting slowly toward us. He said musingly, "Maybe they think they can knock out Fanny."

"I happen to know the geosynch is only a relay," I said. "Fanny is really on Up-Top, the space platform."

"How do you know that?"

"I was up there once. Visiting."

"Don't be so damn smug," Alex said. He let go a soft snort and gave my shoulder a light punch. "Just because you know people in high places."

That wasn't deserving of an answer, so I ignored it. My father (deceased, plane crash) had owned the engineering firm that designed Up-Top. A couple of times he'd taken me up with him. All I remembered were long curving corridors and the wonderful phenomenon of weightlessness.

Lieutenant Barnes chose that moment to climb up the ladder a step or two and peer at us both.

"You're both breaking regulations," he said with a mocking shake of his head. He quoted: " 'Observation vehicles shall be "buttoned up" during hostilities.' "

"There's no more firing," Alex pointed out. "Hostilities are over. Fanny bloodied their noses."

"True enough." He regarded us for a moment. "But HQ is sending down a senior field man. And I suggest we follow regs until he leaves."

The Observation Vehicle was thirty-one feet long, twelve wide. Its interior was built along the lines of a self-contained sloop. There was just enough room for the engines, us four rats, and the several thousand miles of circuitry that linked Obscon-27 to the onboard computer and thence to the geosynch. There was *some* armament fore and aft, but it was more cosmetic than not.

In the command station, Colonel John Phillips looked us over with a faint-subtle-nasty stare. He was a small man, with the Napoleonic air some small men generate. He stared longest at Alex, craning his neck back and studying the bottom of the signalman's chin.

"There's going to be a push," he said, redirecting his stare toward Barnes. "The enemy has moved in ten units, and there are two aircraft carriers heading into the Gulf of Guinea."

"What's their Control, sir?" Barnes asked.

Phillips grinned tightly. "A Sololief 20. Bigger, faster, and better than anything they've had up to now."

Barnes gave a silent whistle. The present Soviet war computer was a Sololief 4, a relatively primitive model that'd been updated from time to time.

"That Twenty," Barnes said, staring somberly at Phillips, "you think it can really beat Fanny Six?"

The colonel squared his jaw. "I don't know, Lieutenant. But I expect we'll find out damn soon." He turned his head, looking at each of us. "When the push *does* come, we'll be looking to you for on-site information." He paused for the length of time it took to stroke his pencil-thin moustache and grin. "After all, nothing beats an observer in the field."

Colonel Phillips interviewed each of us privately, using Barnes's tiny cabin as an office. Dockrats are known to be unhinged, else why would we volunteer for Obscon duty. Phillips wanted to know if we were sufficiently unhinged to stay put when enemy rockets were zeroing in.

When my turn came I eased past Pete Stillus, making sure my brass was in place and my shirttail tucked in.

Pete grabbed my arm and looked apprehensive. "Phillips must have had crocodile for breakfast—and he's been asking questions about you. Watch out for him."

"Questions—about me?" I shook my head, puzzled, then slipped on by and opened the door. Phillips was standing with his back to me, studying a map of the Niger Valley.

He turned around as I entered, looked at me for maybe five seconds, then sat down behind Lieutenant Barnes's desk. He extracted a file from an attaché case and took his time scanning it.

"So you're Gilliam Warren," he said. He put the file down and fingered the chunk of blue quartz Barnes kept as a paperweight.

"Yes, sir."

"All this true?" he asked, stabbing a finger toward the file.

"All what, sir?"

"Don't give me that innocent crap!" He looked angry enough to take a bite out of the paperweight, but it was all on the surface. No color had reached his cheeks, and his eyes remained speculative. He said, "Is it true you've turned down your past three promotions?"

"Yes, sir."

"And refused an officer's rank?"

"Yes, sir."

He flipped through the report, taking his time. Then he glanced up and closed the file disgustedly.

"It says here that you were a juvenile delinquent, fought with your foster parents, were a perennial runaway. What's the matter, Warren, can't you adjust to society?"

"Those were . . . difficult times for me, Colonel."

He looked at me scornfully. "You think you're the only one had difficult times?"

"No, sir."

He adjusted his cap slightly, stared up at me. "Maybe all that carried over to the military, Warren. Maybe that explains some things we've been wondering about."

"What things, sir?"

He shrugged angrily, laid his arms flat on the desk. "Near insubordination, lack of ambition. You're a goddamn Army misfit, Warren, that's what."

I said nothing, only looked straight over his head.

"Did you ever stop to think of your future here, Sergeant?"

"Not really, sir."

"Why not?"

"Well . . ." I stopped and considered. Going at it this way might mean Phillips was something other than just a field officer. He was playing it a little too cute.

I waited a bit and said instead, "Are you with the Psychological Unit, sir?"

He said no and slammed the paperweight down hard, but he'd hesitated too long. He knew it and I knew it.

He said, "Goddamn you, Warren! You're too valuable to waste yourself on Obscon missions."

I was silent. I stood at ease and waited for his next words. We suddenly lurched and there was a subdued roar as the engines caught. Fanny Six was moving us somewhere. Orders from Geosynch.

Phillips looked uneasy for a second, but he recovered quickly enough. He leaned forward, hands flat on the desk. "It never bothers you, not knowing where you're going?"

"No." I shrugged, feeling Obs-27 banking left, toward Mount Baguezane. Maybe Fanny was going to set us down in the shade somewhere.

Phillips picked up the file again, leafed through several pages, flicked a glance my way. "You were in the infantry for a year. Fought in the battle of Agadem, received a medal for meritorious service."

It hadn't been a question so I didn't reply.

He turned another page. "Before that you were a cryptographer in the Signal Corps. But only for a single tour." He flipped more pages, a disgusted look growing on his face. "Why, Warren? Two and a half years in the Army and you've had nine different MOS's. You have itchy feet or what?" He looked at me with belligerence.

I said, "Colonel, I have six months to go on my enlistment. I'm not staying in the service. So why should anyone care—"

"Because, damn it!" He started to say something else, stopped when Obs-27 swung in a sudden circle and dropped—like a stone. Presently we were on the ground again, motors off, the guts of the vehicle once more tomblike and silent.

"Jesus!" Phillips said. He looked more than a little green.

"Nobody programmed Fanny to take it easy on passengers," I said. "Far as it knows, we aren't even here."

"That's the whole point," Phillips said. Give him

that, he recovered quickly. "A war computer can't be concerned about field personnel—not if it wants to win a war."

I shrugged.

The chunk of blue quartz had bounced off the ceiling and split neatly in two. Phillips picked up the pieces and put them in a desk drawer.

"It wouldn't matter," he said, looking my way again, "about your enlistment, except that a routine computer run showed a virtual duplication." He selected another file from his attaché case. "You know Chester Markham—in Obscon-25?"

"Yes, sir."

He took a cigarette out of a thin case and lit it, blew smoke toward the ceiling. "He's your half-brother, isn't he?"

"Yes, sir." No point in not telling him, he could verify it easily enough.

He sucked on the cigarette, nodded, smiled a little. "How're you related?"

I said evenly, "My father was Dean Markham. I'm illegitimate, Chester's not—if it matters."

"Ah!" Phillips swiveled back and forth in his chair, looked wise. His moustache twitched.

He said, "That would be the same Dean Markham who built Up-Top?"

"That's right."

"You close, your half-brother and you?"

"You could say so."

"Why are you and he pulling this 'twin' act?"

I sighed. It didn't matter much if he knew; both Mark (he hated Chester) and I would be out of the military inside six months. I said, "It was my father's idea. His will was very particular. It stipulated that we both get a 'well-rounded' education, which was to include one enlistment in the Army."

Phillips took a long, even drag on his cigarette and then put it out. He looked like he didn't believe me.

"He also stipulated," I went on, "that the conditions of the will are to remain confidential. I trust you'll respect that request."

"Oh, come on, Warren! You expect me to believe a cockamamie story like that?"

"It's the truth, Colonel. Dean Markham was a man with peculiar ideas. One of them was that an education isn't over til you've done the old Eskimo bit."

"Being . . .?"

I said, "It involves fighting a bear, drinking whiskey, and making love to an Indian woman. The idea is to know enough not to get them seriously mixed up. He was using it as a metaphor."

"Well, the metaphor escapes me," Phillips began caustically. He stood up and squared his shoulders. At that moment Obs-27 did a 180-degree turn and rose like it was on rockets. I grabbed a bulkhead stanchion and held on.

"We got troubles," Lieutenant Barnes broke in on the intercom. "Gil, get to your station!"

"Roger." I took one look at Colonel Phillips sprawled on the floor and then bolted out the door. He didn't look hurt, but he wouldn't be conducting interviews for a while.

We were flying a funny zigzag pattern that was new to me. I buckled in, flicked on the cameras, and took a look.

We were three hundred feet off the desert floor; in the camera's eye it was nothing but brown blur.

"Take a look over to the right," Alex called out. His elongated frame was hunched over the communication console.

I took a look. It seemed the Eastern Bloc was making their push a lot sooner than Colonel Phillips had anticipated. There were a couple of dozen platform hovers out there, and they didn't belong to our side.

Fanny jinked us right and dropped us fifty feet. As I adjusted the cameras I reflected upon the uncanny powers that we'd invoked in Man's name. Perhaps it was significant that we'd built a war computer to ride around the heavens, a silicon demigod. But, on the other hand, why *not* let the empty war chariots fight each other. Hell—anybody would have to admit it was more practical than the unholy carnage we'd practiced on each other since the dawn of time. Sooner or later everybody would have to face it—the age of the foot soldier was about over. *The charge of the* last *brigade. . . .*

Once again Fanny took charge. This time she turned us end over end and headed straight for the hovers.

"Jesus!" Alex grabbed onto the edge of the console. Lieutenant Barnes was staring into the CRTs, a worried look on his face.

"The rest of the Subcoms are pulling back," Pete Stillus yelled from below. "What in the hell are *we* still doing here?"

"We're being sacrificed—I think," Alex mourned. He looked more than worried—he looked scared. He tore off his earphones and took Barnes's arm. "Cut us out of the command chain, for Christ's sake!"

"We can't be sure," Barnes said. He shook the other's hand away.

"The hell we can't! Fanny's pulling everything back but us. She needs time and we're giving it."

From the hovers came a bright sparkle of lights. A welcoming flight of rockets. Subcom-27 fired their full inventory in return but took no evasive action.

Barnes slid back the cutoff panel, activated the switch, and sat there with his hand on the lever, sweat dripping off his face.

"Pull it, man! Pull it! Fanny doesn't care about us."

Barnes waited two more seconds, indecision making

his face gray. It was not an easy thing, cutting that umbilical cord. It meant we were committing mutiny. Then something slammed the side of the vehicle and his hand moved reflexively backward. Obs-27 started to fall out of the sky.

Each rat had a part of it. You don't control 27 tons of soon-to-be-scrap with just one pair of hands.

We turned upside down and something brushed my arm. I heard yells. There was a smell like smoke and ozone.

Incredibly, we righted just before we hit. The big blades dug at the air. Deep. Deep. I leaned forward, slapped all the jato switches I could reach, felt their effect on the forward portion of the ship. It was too late, though. A lot too late.

Then—a shock wave . . . an unholy fear of endless darkness . . . and endless darkness.

The smoke and ozone woke me up—that and the giant pulling on my left leg. There were voices too, though, and that didn't make sense.

"They got down fine," someone was saying. "Damnedest thing I ever saw. If the field hadn't been mined they'd have gotten away with it."

The giant tugged my leg again and I sought the darkness.

The next time I came around they were lifting me out of the steel cocoon that was the control room housing.

"Hello, ugly," a familiar voice said.

I peered up; I seemed to be suffering delirium. A big man with heavily muscled shoulders, blond hair, and a scar above his right eye was standing over me.

"Mark?"

"Uh huh. Take it easy."

I said, "You cut out of Obs-25 and came back? Don't you know that's a court martial offense?"

He didn't answer. Instead he laid me on soft cool

grass and started working on my left leg. Or, as realization came to me, what was left of it.

"There's somebody else alive," a voice in back of me announced. "In the cabin. We'll have to cut him out." I heard a faint popping sound as an acetylene torch was lit.

"Colonel Phillips."

"What?" Mark leaned over me.

I said, "Anyone else—besides me and Phillips?"

"No." And he did something to my leg that made the world grow a thousand stars and fade away like fog.

I had been in the hospital for two weeks when Phillips came to see me. He had a black eye and a limp and hadn't lost his crisp "little-general" mannerisms.

He said, "I thought you'd like to know. Your half-brother is *not* being court-martialed."

"Your doing?"

He managed a faint smile. "Well, hell—he did save my life."

"Thanks for helping him."

He was silent for a space. Then he said, "He broke a basketful of rules—including the rule against mutiny. He won't be allowed back aboard an Obscon."

"It won't break his heart."

Phillips lit a cigarette and spent five seconds inspecting the cast on my left leg. "You coming along all right?"

I shrugged as well as I was able. "They say I have enough metal in my leg to be declared a natural resource."

He didn't smile. "They thought you'd lose that leg. Another half hour and you would have."

I said, "That reminds me. I haven't seen Mark since he brought me in."

Phillips fingered the ends of his moustache, then pulled a chair forward and sat down. "We're keeping him occupied. He's taking a series of tests. You will, too, as soon as you're able."

"Tests? What tests?"

Instead of answering, he said, "*You* won't be going back to an Obscon position, either."

I repeated what I'd said earlier in regard to Mark. No heartburn.

He said, "But you still have six months of service—and your security clearance."

"So?"

He regarded the ash on his cigarette as though it was the first time he'd seen it. Obliquely, he said, "Ever hear of telekinesis?"

"Moving objects around with the force of your mind?"

"Yes." He got up, stubbed out the cigarette, and took a position by the window. I had to strain my neck to see him. "That computer scan I told you about on Obs-27 was a check on certain test scores you took when you were enlisting."

"It shows I have telekinesis?" I was frankly disbelieving.

"It shows you might have latent ability," Phillips replied with a shrug. "There's a research program going on right now. If you're interested, I think I can get you in."

I mulled it over while Phillips lit another cigarette and contributed in a minor way to the room's air pollution. If he was sincere, it meant I could end my enlistment without getting shot at. Maybe that was what I needed, a nice quiet job in research.

"Sure," I said, straining my neck again. "I'm your man."

"Fine. See me when you're ambulatory." He exited the room without even looking back at me.

A week before I walked out of the hospital (on crutches), an attorney from the firm of Spellman, Kurst, Hitchman and Loring appeared at my bedside and announced that the next installment of monies had been added to my trust fund.

I hadn't seen this one before. His name was Fowler. He was youngish, with long brown sideburns and a sharp, pointed nose. He showed me a book full of figures, itemized debentures, tax-free bonds, and the remainder of investments making up a small portfolio. It wouldn't make me a millionaire, but it was an impressive total nonetheless.

"How long now?" I asked him.

"Our firm will turn the trust over to you, in . . ." he consulted a calendar watch, "four months and fifteen days. On your twenty-fifth birthday."

I gave him a grin. "I'll be on your doorstep."

Book One

Chapter One

If you've never heard of Psychological Phase States you've never heard of Fred Sandone. That is no great loss in itself; his personality is loaded with emotional barbwire. I've known moray eels with more charm.

Take nothing from the man—brilliance has been visited upon him. His words sing with nonpareil depth and weight. He stands upon the shoulders of giants and is as a giant himself. He probably knows more about the human brain than any man alive.

When we were first introduced he merely looked at me, pushing his hornrim spectacles back with one blunt fingertip.

"Why are you on crutches?"

I could have said "because I don't want to fall down," but I didn't. Instead, I said, "The African 'police action.' Colonel Phillips said there was some urgency or I'd still be at home. What *is* the hurry, anyway?"

"Don't ask too many questions, Warren." He glowered a little. "But I'll tell you this much. What we do here may have an effect on the 'police action' you mentioned."

He gave me tests—written, oral, physical, mental.

Then he went away and left me sitting in the murky half-light of the examination room. Twenty minutes later he came back and tapped me painfully on the shoulder.

"Be here at seven o'clock tomorrow." He pronounced it like a sentence, as an angry judge might.

I was there at seven o'clock the next morning, and for many mornings after.

The mind is a funny thing. It's full of little hidden corners and cul-de-sacs. It's mostly unexplored country, and there are damn few maps. Give credit to Sandone; he's as good a cartographer as ever I've seen.

His laboratory was simply a green tiled room with lots of glass and sculptured modern furniture that made you itch for something substantial in walnut and oak; it was about thirty feet square.

The center of the room was taken up by a large day couch—very plush, very comfortable. I lay down on the couch and Sandone sat in one of the sculptured chairs just out of my sight. Someone gave me an injection.

The lights dimmed. A technician named Toby came trundling in with the bio-feedback machinery. After a while there were metallic sentinals all around me, solemn and sedate.

"In a few moments," Sandone told me, "I'm going to create a state of hyperaesthesia. Just relax and do as I say."

He was very thorough. It was the forty-second time I'd lain on that couch.

As it was explained to me, Sandone isolated a tiny slice of my consciousness. He marked it so that he wouldn't lose it, then set up perimeters and staked it off. Pretty soon he built a high fence. Very carefully, he began to carry out irrelevant material and throw it over the fence. Once he was reasonably sure there were no hidden pockets of contamination, he began to cart in material from the outside—fluids with names ending in—mine, and—ide. He was very skillful with his chemical tongs; I hardly knew he was there.

Access to this little playground of the subconscious was through a key made up of physical and mental sets. Sandone had been down this road before, with four different subjects. One of them, I had found out earlier, was Mark. My half-brother, it seemed, had significant telekinetic ability.

Afterwards Sandone gave me the standard guff about resting until my headache went away. The way he said it, bristling with barnacles, I guessed that sometime, somewhere, someone had given him an ugly time.

"Beer?"

The technician, name of Toby Roberson, bobbed his head. I signaled the pretty barmaid for two more drafts.

The bar was five or six blocks from Sandone's laboratory, a quiet comfortable place with boxers' pictures on the wall and a stained-glass door. I had seen Toby enter and curiosity made me follow. Like everybody else at Sandone's lab, he had seemed uncommunicative—at first. With two or three beers in him he seemed friendlier.

"You getting around any better?" he asked me, nodding at the cane I'd hung on the bar rail.

"Much," I said. The cane was a symbol, I thought. And damn soon I'd be getting rid of it.

"I read your medical report," he commented dourly. "You were being measured for a prosthetic."

"Lucky me."

He drank from the beer stein, put it down, lighted a small black cigarillo. Toby had some peculiar ideas on the meaning of life. One time in the lab I'd come across him reading a book on the zen of near-death experiences. His taste in things was not macabre, yet . . .

"Have you worked for Sandone long?" I asked.

"A year or two."

"You really think he can turn us into telekinetic . . ." I said, and fumbled for the noun.

"Telekines," he supplied immediately, and looked at me. "Sure. I've seen it happen. Scary, the first time. Not anymore, though."

I looked at the wet rings my beer stein had left on the bar, said, "How can our research here have anything to do with the African stalemate?"

He didn't answer for a long time. When he did it was with a resigned shake of his head. "Damn world might blow any minute. All it needs is a spark, maybe a little friction. And it doesn't *have* to be Africa—that's just the likeliest spot at the moment." He shrugged and emptied the stein past the halfway point. "Telekines might make the difference."

I said, "Is it true that misfits seem to make the best subjects? I saw a paper on Sandone's clipboard about murderers and sociopaths."

Toby placed the stein against his forehead for the cool of it. "That seems to be true enough. In fact, one of the subjects is a . . ." And he stopped and let it lie.

"A murderer?"

He shook his head and looked past my shoulder. "You didn't hear it from me."

It was unsatisfying, but it would have to do. Toby was not one who became overly loquacious.

In my apartment, with the lights dimmed so that just the Rembrandt copy glowed in its shrine, I poured myself a tumbler of Scotch and laid me down to think.

After a while I got up, hit the stud that opened the french windows, and let the autumn wind surge over me, savoring the mountain tastes and factory wastes. Pittsburgh at twilight. There was a corona flash of red in the western sky and I watched one of the shuttles slide down from Up-Top. I saluted it—and the city—

with the Scotch before reentering the apartment and dogging the doors.

I picked up the phone and called Mark. I had seen him twice since he'd scraped up what was left of me out there on the Niger plain. Like me, he'd suffered Sandone's attentions. On occasion, we had talked about the Phase State program, tossing ideas back and forth, trying to figure out exactly what was going on. We'd never come up with any satisfactory answers. We both seemed to have latent telekinetic ability, though, and that suggested a genetic trait. In the interim, he'd passed my father's Eskimo test. Now my half-brother, six months older than I, was busy managing his mini-fortune.

"Mark!"

"Hello, ugly," he said. He gave me a grin.

I held up a little black card embossed with white lettering so that he could see it.

"Got an invitation to attend the opening of the Warmath Museum."

"I know," he said. "I arranged it. I thought you liked Warmath."

"I did. I do. I didn't know you had that kind of clout."

He grinned more widely. "Well, don't spread it around. Anyway, this is supposed to be one of Warmath's crazier efforts. By the way, is Sandone about finished with you?"

"Will be in two more sessions. He thinks maybe he's misplaced a few of the marbles."

"How many sessions will that make?"

"Forty-four."

Mark whistled. "He's never done that many on any-one. He finished up on me after thirty-six."

We reminisced a little, then hung up, and I went into the little kitchenette to freshen my Scotch. I dug around in the tumble of books until I found *Warmath on Warmath*.

I suppose genius is a word that has been as overworked as any other. In Roman antiquity the word meant either of two attendant spirits, one good, one bad, who accompanied a person through life. That being so, Warmath's were demon and angel, fire and ice, darkness and light, purity and carnality.

Early in his career, he'd worked exclusively with copper and glass, creating explosions in form and perspective. Gradually he had worked his way down the mediums to simple clay.

He was now resurgent, and all his latest works were done in brass, hand cast in the classic style.

Even as overworked as it has become, there is no better word to describe the man. Genius.

Of course I'm fickle. I say the same thing about Rembrandt.

I closed the book and stood up, finishing my Scotch.

In the bathroom, I turned the water on hot and stood under it while the aches left my bad left leg. As I climbed out I studied my reflection in the mirror and made a face. It was hard to recognize the slightly battered creature looking back at me. A little over average height, skinny, with coarse black hair; scars here and there; thick eyebrows like reversed hooks over slightly reddened eyes. Not the picture I carried in my mind's eye.

The next morning there was news of an African settlement. I phoned the laboratory and they said it was so but no scheduling was changed and to report at the usual time.

I had breakfast at the open pavilion in front of the new library. Eggs, bacon, a couple of pieces of too-dry toast. I topped it off with a cup of rich Turkish coffee.

The library had been built by computer architecture—which means they plugged in what they wanted, and

took what they got. And in some ways it wasn't bad, if
you liked your buildings both medieval and modern.
The computer had selected apple trees and ivy in its
landscape motif. It had probably used a mutate, since
everywhere you looked there were green leaves. I had
the feeling that if I stayed for a second cup of coffee
they'd find me a year later, my bones gaily entwined
with the stuff.

From the pavilion I could see the faint black ribbon
(in reality a fifteen–foot wall) that marked the plague
park. Mark up another one for the military. They'd let
a biological genie out of the bottle and hadn't been able
to get it back in again. At the exact center of the park
was a laboratory where they'd been experimenting on
recombinant DNA for military purposes. They said sec-
tions of the park were livable now, but no one has gone
there to find out.

The autumn winds were kicking up a fuss along the
streets, driving little dust devils to and fro. A fat man
got out of his electric half a block away and his hat
immediately sailed off his head and down the street.

Sandone was waiting for me at the laboratory. The
room never changed; not a speck of dust showed on the
glass surfaces. Sandone never changed, either. He
glanced up from a clipboard and indicated with his eyes
that I was to take a chair.

"You're late," he said.

"Only a bit. Besides, with the African thing being
settled, we should have more time."

Sandone just looked at me. He was not a big man,
but he gave an impression of largeness. He wore a pair
of thick glasses that made his eyes appear like blue
searchlights.

He pushed a button on the console beside him and a
moment later Toby came in, pulling his little train of
bio-equipment. As usual, he had the cart with the bell
jar.

When all the sensors had been taped to my scalp, chest, and hands, Toby rolled the bell jar into place before me.

"You know the sets," Sandone said. "Begin whenever you're ready."

The bell jar was set over a stainless steel plate. On the plate was a small metal ball, no larger than a pea. I looked at Sandone, who looked back at me without expression.

I'd been trying to move that ball off and on for a week without success. I wondered who would give up first, me or Sandone.

Without even trying I slid into the proper set. I didn't have to look at the bio-feedout to know my brain waves were hitting eighteen cycles per second in the beta range, and my physical numbers were right in line. My eyes became glued to the little metal ball, willing it to move. It didn't. And after fifteen minutes, it hadn't.

"That's enough," Sandone said. He touched my shoulder.

"Sorry." There was no feeling of fatigue, nothing but a generalized dissatisfaction.

Sandone cut me short and I moved to the day couch, hundreds of me reflected in the panes of polished glass. A moment later I felt the sharp bite of the hypodermic. I looked up and saw Sandone thumbing his recorder. "Session forty-three," he said in a growling voice.

There was a lot that went on, while Sandone poked and prodded down there in that lens of consciousness he was building.

It was on two levels.

Part of it was like having a dentist fussing with a tooth—he's seen from strange and terrible angles, doing things of which you know not. After a while your attention strays, and you are aware of him only peripherally, touching and daubing, picking and polishing. The remainder of your attention is diverted to other things.

My attention wandered in the labyrinth that was my mind.

First of all, there was sound, a faint chirruping click that had no source. Everything was cast green, and a host of unconnected pictures made a ghost's parade across my inward vision.

A totally different Sandone loped into view, smiled warmly, pressed my arm in reassurance, and grinned a grin filled with chalky teeth.

"This is the real me," he said. "The one up there is a fake."

"I'm happy to hear that."

He took a green metal ball from his pocket and hung it in midair about chin-high.

"Knock it down, Gilliam."

"Can't."

"Go ahead, give it a try."

The ball did a little bounce and then zoomed straight up out of sight. Sandone looked pleased. "Good work." He patted me on the back.

"Aw—it's nothing."

He beamed at me, pulled off his glasses and threw them away, revealing eyes like rain-washed skies and robin's eggs. The searchlights went skittering wildly through the green.

"Hang in there, Gilliam," he said, and began to grow smaller.

"You too," I said. A rope suddenly appeared and I grabbed on, letting it pull me up—up to where Sandone was snapping his fingers to bring me awake.

"Get up," he said, sheathing his words in quicklime.

I stood up, dangling wires and sensors. Toby plucked them off and stashed them on their proper carts. Sandone was already halfway out of the room when I edged my way around the encephalograph. My eyes fell on the bell jar and without thinking I slid into the proper set.

The tiny round ball did not move, though I suddenly felt I had pushed a boulder several yards up a sixty-degree incline.

Chapter Two

Ah, well, what can you say about a Warmath party?

I entered the museum through darkness, tiny pin-pricks of light dancing to show me where to put my feet. Maids in ramhorn helmets came strutting to show me through the cymbaling bronze doors.

"I'm *so* glad to see you," a beautiful woman said.

I grinned at her, proferring my white-on-black invitation. There was a tramp, tramp, tramp as a dozen waiters went by with drinks and canapés and other comestible delights. All around me were the elite of the elite, their women draped in sequins and sapphires, their flesh pooling white-white and brown-brown in the light of a hundred torches.

One of the maids, seeing me standing alone, smiled and nestled in my arm.

"Who is that?" I asked, pointing toward the woman. She was greeting other arrivals, her breasts and coiffure bobbing welcome.

"You really mean you don't know? Where have you *been*? That's Frances Willow. Isn't she lovely?"

I remembered the name. The latest rage. She was discovered dancing naked in a theatre in Soho.

Two minstrels in motley came strolling, pan pipes and ukelele blending in thready harmony.

In the center of the great room was a roped off area, some immensity beneath it covered by a velvet drop-cloth. Warmath's creation.

I saw Mark, carried my maid with me to meet him.

"Avery Fannon is here," Mark said. He grinned in a silly fashion and his eyes gleamed. "And his daughter. Have you seen Alicia Fannon?"

"No."

"She'll knock your eyes out. I want you to meet them both. You know Fannon's big in war computers and . . ."

"I know," I said. "His company—one of them, at least—built Fanny VI."

Mark nodded, put his arm around my shoulder, gave me a hug reminiscent of an anaconda. My maid vanished back into the melee. Clearly excited, Mark said, "Little brother, you have no idea of the power of a man's personality until you meet Avery Fannon. Energy jumps off him like goddamn sparks!"

"You sound as though you like him."

I got a nod. "Enough to work with him—Up-Top."

"You've been up there?" I cocked an eye.

"Uh huh." Mark let me go, took a sip of his drink.

"What are you doing—up there?"

"Can't tell you."

We had known each other since boyhood. Mark had always been bigger, stronger, more of an extrovert. Neither of us, oddly, looked like our father, though Mark came nearer than I.

The crowd swirled, and suddenly Mark said, "Hey, there he is now!" He waved at a figure in unrelieved black, and Avery Fannon excused himself and came toward us.

"Mr. Fannon, my brother, Gil Warren."

We shook hands and Fannon's eyes glinted into mine. He had a raw charm, great intensity. I began to understand what Mark meant. Being next to Fannon was like rubbing shoulders with a large and potentially fierce wild animal.

He said, "Happy to meet you. I don't know if Chester has told you, but I've appropriated his services."

"He mentioned it just a moment ago."

Mark seemed mesmerized by Fannon. Easy to get hooked by that animal charisma, I guessed. Fannon said to me, "There might be a place for you, too, now that the African thing's been settled."

"Oh?"

Before I said more Julius Warmath made his triumphal entrance.

A huge pair of swing doors opened at the other end of the room. A trio of spotlights fell upon four yoked water buffaloes pulling a ten-foot carriage. A boy in a coolie hat beat at the buffaloes' flanks while inside the carriage Warmath waved to one and all. On both sides of the carriage came short-skirted girls throwing flowers. Everything was painted a rich leprechaun green.

As they neared the center of the room, where the velvet dropcloth obscured his creation, Warmath rose in the carriage and doffed his hat, showing himself to be an impostor. Immediately he was whisked into the air on hidden wires. The spotlights left him and fell upon the coolie, who removed his hat and revealed the wide impish grin and bald head so widely known as Warmath's trademarks.

"He's done it again!" a voice said from behind me.

Now conducting an invisible orchestra, Warmath coaxed a crescendo from the minstrels. The velvet lifted on hidden wires and the spotlights converged.

I felt chills engulf me. Silence fell upon the revelers. The music came tumbling downhill and rested in single plunked notes upon the floor.

The scene was from mythology: Chiron the Centaur being instructed by Apollo and Diana. One hand held a caduceus, the other a spear. The huge brass figures seemed supercharged with energy.

With a lithe movement Frances Willow mounted the platform and patted Apollo naughtily. Hidden speakers carried her voice fluting over us in a fountain of sound.

"Ladies and gentlemen! This sculpture, entitled simply *Centaur,* is Julius Warmath's latest contribution to the arts and will reside permanently here in the museum. It is the first *kinetic* sculpture ever made. Over the next twenty years the figures will change subtly and assume new positions. Even as you watch, the sculpture is changing—though so slowly you are unaware of it. Ladies and gentlemen, I give you *Centaur*—and Julius Warmath!"

The spotlights left her and fell upon the little artist, who jumped nimbly up on the platform and scaled his coolie hat into the air. He was about to speak when the pair of swing doors opened again and all heard a bugle sound *charge.* A troop of blue-clad cavalry came charging through, sabres held at the ready, regimental banner forward and high. As they charged by, two of them scooped up Warmath, one on each arm, and exited—with the sculptor facing rear, his short legs making absurd running motions.

Laughter.

Applause.

Mark cleared his throat. "What can you say after *that*?"

"He's a clown," Fannon said. His eyes dismissed *Centaur* after a few seconds. His gaze met mine, fell away, came to rest on a young woman with auburn hair and rakehell green eyes.

"You haven't met Alicia," he said to me.

The girl had been entranced by the spectacle. "Oh, father, that was a bravura performance—and you know it!" She turned her eyes on me and I no longer wondered why Mark had worn a silly grin.

*   *   *

Outside the apartment windows the winds were blowing leaves around; they made a dry, rustling, scratching sound against the glass. I opened the french windows and let some of them in. I breathed deeply and caught glimpses of the lemon-colored moon around the ragged dipping curtains.

The party had been over for hours.

There was a knock at the door. When I opened it Mark was standing there, his blond hair tousled from the wind.

"Come on in," I said.

"You're alone, I hope."

"Matter-of-fact."

"Good. Hate to interrupt anything."

Inside the room, he stood frowning at the Rembrandt and the open french windows. With a shrug I hit the stud and left the wind outside. He would have to suffer *The Night Watch*. He collapsed into a chair and I went into the kitchenette to make him a drink. By the time I returned he had made himself comfortable.

"Did Fannon offer you a position with Fannon Enterprises?"

"Not in so many words, but I got the idea something like that was in the wind. Why do you ask?"

He drank off a goodly portion of the Scotch. "He's employed everyone in the Phase State project, did you know that? All four of us work for Avery Fannon."

"I guess I'm missing the point," I said.

"The point is that Fannon wants you, too, after Sandone is finished with you."

"What does Fannon know about Phase States?"

"Just about everything," Mark answered. "He's financing the whole thing."

"Oh!"

"Thought you'd be impressed. Also, if you're available, he wants me to take you Up-Top tomorrow."

"The space platform?"

"That's right."

I poured myself a drink. "Go on."

"I've only been working up there a few weeks my-self." Mark slung a leg over the chair arm, glanced at me. His face was animated, suffused with something close to . . . joy. I had never seen him look that way. "Fannon has built a new computer up there, linked it into something he calls the Babylon Gate."

"Never heard of it."

"You will," Mark assured me. He grinned and raised his glass in a mock toast.

I said, "I skimmed Who's Who and Barrons. Fannon is not just 'Fannon,' he's Fannon of Fannon Enter-prises. Principal wealth was obtained through war com-puters, pharmaceuticals, and gold mines. Six years ago he leased one third of Up-Top."

"The Babylon Gate is going to make all that wealth seem like nothing at all," Mark replied. He finished the Scotch and stood up. At the door he turned and said, "Don't get any ideas about Alicia. I'm staking that out for myself."

"Perish the thought," I said.

At three o'clock in the morning, I was still awake, prowling around the apartment, contentment and sleep giving way to a restless stirring of memories. I felt a heavy headache coming on and dosed myself with aspi-rin before going to the bathroom and spending twenty minutes under the shower. After that I had another small drink and fell across the bed, sleep coming even before my head touched the pillow.

Back when I was completing a college course in psychology, I ran across Jung's relationship between dreams and alchemy. It reminded me of Sandone and the improbable thing he was doing inside my head. Sometimes, obedient to Sandone's will—resin, fret, and horsehair wailing his song—I was tempted to question him on his choice of me as instrument.

In my dream, I met a Sandone different from either of the two I'd met before. This one had Sandone's thick glasses, wide squat stance, and searchlight gaze. His face, however, was that of Fannon. I had impressions of soft, almost white eyelashes, slightly slanted eyes of cold blue, a tiny frigid white moustache.

In the dream, Sandone-Fannon walked widdershins about a square lined and ruled and peopled with dark unfathomable chess pieces. Here a rook, its gothic crenelated tower looming high; over there a paladin, struck from Warmath's genius—a centaur. Frozen in brass, it longs for freedom, strains for release to skim the plain. Still further into shadow was a menacing faceless bishop, his mitre a dull oblong.

As I recalled, Jung analyzed such a square as a symbol of alchemic work in progress, eventually resulting in a circle, or mandala. In my dream, Sandone-Fannon walked his short-legged walk, grinding his teeth and tugging at something beyond my view. Whatever it was, it terrified me.

I awoke to a new autumn day. The wind had quieted, and a foggy softness and leafy quiet was settled on the world outside my apartment.

I called the laboratory and told them I was going Up-Top and to postpone my final session with Sandone. When I called Mark he answered wearing a face that had seen too little sleep, too much booze, and maybe too much of Alicia Fannon. He grunted at me like a great blond ape, then pulled himself together and said to meet him at the shuttle terminal in two hours.

I got to the terminal long before Mark did. I had a leisurely breakfast of synthetic ham and ersatz barley cakes and read a paper some other commuter had left lying on the counter.

The African settlement had run into a snag. Though hostilities had ceased, so had negotiations.

A dam had given way in upper Oregon, flooding half a dozen downstream towns and leaving thousands homeless. President Dodd had declared the state a disaster area.

The Apollo Observatory on the moon's dark side reported the approach of a very small comet.

The Yankees made hash out of Lehnhart's third attempt at twenty victories. He had allowed twelve hits, two of them home runs, before being lifted in the sixth inning. The Yankees had gone on to whip Boston eleven to one.

I was just finishing the crossword puzzle when Mark arrived. With a shave and a few cups of coffee he more closely resembled the Mark I knew. He grinned weakly and waved two tickets.

"Shuttle's leaving in fifteen minutes," he said.

The trip up was uneventful. The shuttle was a combined-form plane and rocket. Long ago, when the shuttle was first employed, they'd stuck it piggyback atop a regulation aircraft, then atop a rocket. The combined form simply eliminated the two stages. The shuttle ran on jets to a certain height and then switched to rocket power.

The Platform looked stately and sedate, seen through the scanner ports. Its circular motion could plainly be discerned and it flickered like a thousand-faceted diamond against the outflung open pit of space. It grew immense, until it occluded the sky. We passed hundreds of mirrored vanes. Sometime later we fell into shadow, became an axle, and matched spin with the Platform. There were faint sucking sounds at the airlocks. The blue disembark sign flickered on, in three languages. I got a friendly smile from one of the stewardesses before Mark nudged me out of my seat.

"Come on, we're expected," he said. He handed me

a blue card with a clip attached and I stuck it on my shirt. He attached a similar identification to his own jacket and waved me along.

The Babylon Gate Complex occupied an entire ring of the Platform. Heavy electrical cables ran everywhere like fossilized snakes, and there was a raw unfinished quality about things.

There were several rooms on the other corridor that *were* finished, however. One of them had walls of rubbed walnut, and the carpet had a pile at least an inch thick. A huge kidney-shaped desk of dark marble occupied one end.

With a baronial smile, Avery Fannon rose from the desk and waved us in.

"Welcome to the Babylon Gate," he said with old-fashioned courtesy. He indicated chairs and we sat. Like the evening before, he was clad in unrelieved black, an affectation that contrasted dramatically with his near-albino eyebrows.

He made a gesture with his palms up. His smile was warm, full of that irrepressible Fannon charm. "My own trifle of a toy. It's linked through a Fannon VII computer."

"I didn't know there *was* a Fanny seven," I said.

"It's the prototype," Fannon responded equably. "Hence the ongoing work—they're still installing parts of it. It's years ahead of anything commercially—or even militarily—available."

"And it's going to run the Babylon Gate—whatever that is?"

"Indeed. And we'll get to that." Fannon flicked a toggle on his desk. One wall vanished, giving me the feeling that I was about to be sucked out into space. He flicked another toggle, and a planet bloomed in the emptiness. Mars.

"Computer analogue," Fannon grunted. He did something to his console and Mars grew until it filled the screen—or until we had fallen to within a mile or so of its surface. Fannon did some fine-tuning and we fell more slowly, until finally we floated as gently as butterflies just above the plain. Red dust was everywhere.

I drew in a deep breath. "That's very impressive," I said. "You could make a fortune with that at an amusement center."

Fannon did not comment. He lit a cigar and settled back in his chair, his glance sweeping across that red surface.

"I want Mars," he said. "The Earth is getting crowded. *Too* crowded. Now, if we dig for copper ore in Michigan, we have to relocate thousands of residents. If we irrigate the Sahara, we have to steal the water from someone else."

Exhaling a blue plume of smoke, he did things to the console and Mars began to change, writhing in the computer's grasp. Slowly, the surface took on a new shape. Tiny lichen-like plants rippled in the thin Martian winds. Here a gnarled stump rose, bloomed, and died, all in seconds. Seed was scattered, other stumps rose, and roots bubbled the red surface. The sky cleared of dust and something strange and miraculous happened.

It rained on Mars.

Fannon slapped a switch and stopped the display. The wall shut in against itself, becoming polished wood once more.

"Our objective is to make Mars habitable," Fannon said around his cigar. "The Babylon Gate is designed to do that. It takes ordinary thought and aligns it—focuses it—much as a laser aligns light."

I looked at Fannon. His aura of animal energy almost filled the room, provoking, challenging. He grinned abruptly and I felt like a fly on flypaper.

"Ordinary thought patterns can't do much more than raise dust and move small stones around," Mark said.

"Sandone tried some of the best minds in the country—to no avail."

Fannon bit on the cigar, bounced to his feet. "The answer, damn it, was to train people especially for it. The concentration required is a megajump above anything the average person can generate."

I leaned forward. "Sandone's Phase States!"

"Exactly—" Mark began, but Fannon cut him off, began talking in staccato bursts.

"We tested thousands of people. Exhaustively. Trained them by trial and error. Damned expensive, but hang that! Finally got a few with the proper qualifications—latent psi ability. Required three minimum but luckily got five." He grinned like a sunburst. "Mark?" He tossed a pen onto the desk's gleaming surface.

Mark looked at Fannon, at me, and at the pen that lay on the desk. With a slight shrug he began to concentrate on the pen. His body relaxed and I recognized the moment he went into set. The pen began to move, rolling around the desk in lazy turns. Abruptly it lifted and hovered some inches above the marble surface. It floated over to Fannon, who plucked it out of the air and tucked it into a pocket.

"I envy you," he said to us both. "You'll be building a new world, and history will build statues in your honor—though your real monument will be the red planet itself."

"I don't need to say that this is all confidential," Mark said to me. "There are industrial spies right now trying to buy their way Up-Top. Mr. Fannon has effective means of dealing with them."

I nodded faintly, wondering how rich a toy like this would make Fannon.

"The possibilities are endless," he murmured aloud, as though reading my mind. Then he inclined his head, narrowing his eyes at us. Anguish tightened his mouth. "You don't know how much I wanted to take part in this thing—but my psi tests didn't even make the chart. You two, and the other three, you're the lucky ones."

Briefly, outside in the corridor, Mark took my arm and led me toward an open bay. There were a handful of men there, working on what looked like a demented man's throne.

He didn't have to tell me. The Babylon Gate.

"See those two men there?" he said, and pointed. I followed the direction he indicated. One of the men was huge, bearded, unkempt-looking. The other was of average height, with narrow shoulders and a large head.

"Two of your colleagues," Mark said. "The third has to be around here somewhere. Ah . . ." And he pointed again.

The third telekine was young, maybe eighteen or so. His hair was sunbleached and worn long.

And one of them, I thought, was a murderer.

The trip down was a repeat in reverse of the earlier experience, except that the scanner ports showed us a half-crescent like a cloudy blue pearl.

At the shuttle terminal Mark muttered something about a date and I saw him into a taxi. I wandered for a while, thinking about the Babylon Gate and Fannon, and remembering the Martian light that looked like it had been sifted through fine-mesh silk.

After a couple of hours I called the laboratory, but evening was coming on so I was instructed to report the next day. I took a taxi to the museum and stood in front of Warmath's *Centaur,* sensing the power, the suppressed *elan* of the thing. I recalled that the sculpture was kinetic—in motion—and tried to imagine what Chiron would be up to in the years ahead.

Chapter Three

The news in the morning was all bad. The African settlement had come unraveled. Sides were choosing up again, and it looked like Fannon VI and Sololief Twenty were opponents in earnest. And maybe a little bit more of the world was going to get blown into hell's own cauldron. This time, if not before, they were serious; it looked as though the gloves were coming off.

Sandone did not ask why I hadn't shown up the day before and he didn't comment about the African thing coming apart. He had his clipboard on his lap and he merely grunted at my attempts at conversation.

After a few moments he touched the button on his console, and Toby trucked in with his carts. I dropped into set and threw myself against the weight of that metal pea, moving it not at all. I still felt as though I were trying to roll a five-ton rock up the north side of Pike's Peak.

Sandone touched my shoulder. "Enough. We're going into hyperaesthesia." And I felt the hypo's light sting. Blurrily I heard him activate his recorder.

This time the labyrinth was not green, but a strange powdery red. I recognized it as the Martian surface,

41

and saw devils of sorrel talcum whirling on the far off plain.

I saw a centaur.

He fitted here, his flesh metallic, reflecting a hundred highlights from the distant sun. He grinned crookedly at me, his caduceus dragging in rocky silt, his spear making a fifth leg.

"Hello."

"Hello."

"Are you going to take my world away?"

"Going to change it, is all."

"I like it this way, fella."

"I'm sorry. You see, there's this thing they call the Babylon Gate. . . ."

"I don't want to hear it, bub. Now just buzz off and leave us centaurs in peace, okay?"

"You're not very friendly. I've come all this way to help you out. We can put a lake over there, and there'll be groves of trees around it. There won't be any more dust storms, either."

The centaur gave me a pitying look and stuck his caduceus in a belt I hadn't noticed earlier.

"For generations we've been working to get those dust storms just right," he said, and shook his head. "And now along comes a johnny-come-lately who wants to do away with them." He turned and trotted away, his tail straight up, his spear held canted, like a knight in the lists.

I tried to call him, but something was banging on my head in an annoying fashion. Eventually I recognized Sandone's delicate touch and allowed myself to be pulled awake.

"Okay, now listen," Sandone rasped out. "I've kept certain restraints in place for the past half-dozen sessions. I didn't want you going off half-cocked with this thing and drawing attention to yourself."

"What kind of restraints?"

"Oh, just a mind-block here and there. They've all been taken off now—your preparation is complete." He pointed to the bell jar and Toby trundled it toward me.

I felt more confident this time. I could *feel* the horsepower I was thrusting against that steel ball.

I don't know how much later I realized that the ball was not going to move. Pike's Peak had become the slopes of Everest; the ball gained weight and breadth as I pushed it up that lonesome incline. From somewhere, I could hear the tinny laugh of a Martian centaur.

Sandone was perplexed. He studied the metering readouts and reset the EEG. He glowered at me from wrathful eyes and ordered me to try again.

The tiny metal pea became the center of my universe. I shrugged away the world like peeling off clothes and snugged my shoulder beneath that cold reflective sphere. With the vaunted strength of Atlas I heaved, bending mental legs for better leverage.

Somewhere just short of Everest's summit, I lost it, and came crawling back to Sandone, hat in hand.

There were other tests. Sandone was thorough and dogged. We had reached the point where Sandone's process ought to show the first real proof of kinetic potential—and nothing was happening.

Sandone trotted through his barrel of tricks. It was impressive, but it was in vain. The metal ball sat as though glued to the plate beneath the bell jar.

After three days he threw up his hands.

"I don't understand it!" He hammered a fist against his palm, face twisted angrily. "The indications were on track through every stage. Get out!" He pushed me toward the door, his voice like sandpaper. "Go on, get out!"

Officially, I washed out of the program. Mark came over to commiserate and we went through a bottle or two of Scotch, ending up at a local bar at three in the morning polluted in the finest sense and singing like canaries at the moon. Shortly thereafter, he was called Up-Top and I received a quiet visit from Colonel Phillips. He suggested I forget I'd ever heard of the Babylon Gate.

We were standing on the walk overlooking the Allegheny River, rain falling lightly, the afternoon sky full of haze. Phillips was dressed in a suit instead of a uniform.

He said, "Just regard it as a temporary job—a well-paid one. A large sum has already been deposited with your bank. Two years' pay for an Obscon man." He flicked open an umbrella as he looked at me.

"I'm no longer an Obscon man," I said. "My enlistment ended three weeks ago. I'm a civilian now."

"Well, I wish you luck in civilian life." He turned toward me, smiled, nodded, and then was gone, one more featureless figure on the walk.

I took it hard. I'd wanted to work down there on Mars, changing that implacable face and bringing life where life had never been.

The threat of war became more than a threat. It became all there was. We woke with it in the morning and we went to bed with it at night. It hung over us like a scimitar of doom.

Then I met Catherine.

It was at a class in sculpture I'd been attending at a branch of Penn State University. I badly needed to get my hands into something that would be a balm to my spirit. The clay I pounded and worked took on surrogate status, a vicarious mirroring of the planet fourth from the sun.

If I had been any good, I don't suppose she'd have noticed me. It was because I was so hopelessly inept that she stopped for a few moments to give me pointers.

Her name was Catherine Delaney, and she had a smudge of clay across one cheek. She had light brown hair and gray eyes that twinkled good-humoredly. There were no rings on her fingers or fiances lurking in the background and she knew Julius Warmath personally. Without a glance backward, I fell head over heels in love with the lady.

One morning I awoke and found the trees snow-laden. Autumn had vanished and the winds would now blow cold. Around the heavy traffic lanes the bushrows were white-bearded old men, and the leaves of a season had gone . . . where?

The phone buzzed while I sat sipping a second cup of coffee. When I answered it I found Catherine grinning at me like an impish snowmaiden.

"Morning, Gil. Take a look outside."

"I did. I have. I don't like it. Brrr."

"Oho! Listen, do you still want to meet Julius?"

"Doesn't everybody?"

"Hmm—no. But okay, listen. He has a place up in the Poconos he uses when he wants privacy—or when he wants to lick his wounds. He's invited me up for a few days. Would you like to come along?"

"Yes. Of course. Absolutely. But hold on—maybe he doesn't want strangers barging around."

She grinned again. "Don't worry about that. If you're with me and I like you, that's enough for him."

"Yes, but. . . ."

"Pick you up in an hour?"

"Yeah."

It was a lengthy trip, but the company was pleasant. We ate sandwiches she'd brought along and talked about sculpturing, the length of hemlines, and a potpourri of other things. At one point, however, she gave me a sere look, said, "You don't talk much about yourself, do you?"

I shrugged, leaned back against the soft vinyl. "I'm Dean Markham's bastard son. I was raised by a foster family, one chosen for me."

"And your mother?" Softly.

"She died. Toxemia."

She said nothing for a moment, her hand resting lightly on the electric's yoke. Then she murmured, "You haven't had an easy life, have you?"

"I'm not complaining. Fifteen years ago my father found me. Or remembered me. Since then things have improved." I glanced her way and grinned. "Right now things are *fine!*"

Warmath's retreat was a monstrous stone winter palace with high gabled windows and foot-thick doors. There was a swimming pool in the basement. It was nestled on four hundred acres of virgin wilderness and sky-eclipsing pines.

I had seen the public Warmath, the compleat clown, the *artist artificer*. The man Catherine introduced me to was none of those. He shook my hand politely, and then swallowed Catherine whole in the gnarled hollow of his arm.

"Hello, Cat."

"Hello, Juli." Catherine giggled and managed to kiss the top of Warmath's bald head.

"I've missed you. The old place needs a woman's touch, you know."

"You mean you didn't bring a few up with you this time? Are you slowing down, Juli?"

The artist grinned and slapped her fanny. "This is kind of a special time, Cat. Just me and a few of the things I cherish most."

"Well, show Gil around while I unpack."

"Okay."

Warmath introduced me to Wanda and Aldis Smith, the palace's caretakers. Wanda was a round smiling butterball, and Aldis had the thin ascetic look of a monk. There was also a Great Dane of heroic proportions, and a bevy of snobbish yellow cats.

"Katrinka tells me you're hopeless at sculpting," Warmath said, glancing at me.

"That's true enough."

"She also told me you were at the museum opening."

"That's right. I liked *Centaur*. I've been back several times, studying it, drawn to it."

"Thank you, young man." He looked up at me, pleased.

"I take it you're not going to divulge the sculpture's movements for the next two decades?"

Warmath laughed and waggled his head. "It'd be a real side-slapper if old Chiron's spear ended up in Diana's butt, wouldn't it?"

"That won't happen," I told him.

"No? Why not?"

"You have too much respect for art—for Man."

He peered at me. "Hmm. That's the kind of remark I'd expect from Katie. Expect you're right, too."

Warmath's workshop was an immense room on the third floor of the mansion. He showed me briefly an unfinished sculpture of Catherine—a lifesize nude that all but stepped down and took my hand. The moment I saw it I fell in love with her all over again.

It was a day and a half later that the dark angels of death rustled their wings up and down the land.

In Africa the "last brigade" marched in endless rows, their rifles loaded with contact explosive charges. Mainly, they were aligned with the Eastern Bloc. Fanny VI countered with skimmers armed with air-to-ground missiles, keeping her Subcoms in reserve.

Ultimatums were uttered. Men stood down armed with keys and buttons and blinking maps where soon there would be Armageddon.

The world trembled and waited, and the time for ultimatums passed.

In Warmath's castle we trembled, too, and I held Catherine close in the circle of my arms. Warmath voiced the only sentiment possible, his round face showing disgust. "They're mad! Raving bloody lunatics!"

Sometime later one of the dark angels shrugged, and the first of several missiles shook itself free of the earth and coursed like a fiery arrow toward its target.

Inexplicably it—and those that followed—veered, finally splashed harmlessly into the waters of the Indian Ocean.

The Eastern Bloc brought its Subcoms to bear. Fanny VI parried and retreated.

Miraculously, ahead of the marching armies dams broke, flooding the lowlands. Soldiers threw away their rifles and scrambled for the high ground . . .

Just as miraculously, where there were rivers bridges gave way, crashing into the swollen waters like brittle spider webs . . .

We viewed it all from the ubiquitous darting camera skimmers that wheeled like sparrow hawks above the would-be battlefield.

"What's happening?" Catherine whispered.

Warmath was at a loss. "If I believed in Divine Providence, which I don't, then I'd say He was dissatisfied with the way we were managing things."

I smote my head with a cupped hand. Of course! If the Babylon Gate could change the surface of Mars, it could as easily restructure the epicenters of war.

"It's not Divine Providence," I announced solemnly. And while we watched the nonwar grind to a halt, I told them of the Gate and the whirling Martian sands and the hope of bringing life to that red waste.

Afterwards there was silence. Then Warmath whistled.

"And you say Avery Fannon is in charge up there?"

"That's right."

"We may have climbed out of this kettle into a hotter frying pan, then, son. I've known Fannon for years. Damn megalomaniac! I wouldn't trust him with a day-old beard. And . . . *he's a man who would be king!*"

"Don't worry about that," I said. "He's not alone up there. The telekines are the ones with the real power, and one of them is my half-brother. Mark would never let him take over."

"Fannon isn't easily stopped, once he wants something." Warmath countered with a frown. "And, don't forget, he controls the war computer."

Cold driving snow kept us huddled around the big fireplace while the world learned what we already knew.

It had been several weeks since I'd last tried to move Sandone's metal pea. I tried again, Catherine and Warmath looking on interestedly, the Great Dane nuzzling my face, the cats (as usual) disdaining our company.

Warmath placed a lead sinker on a sheet of paper and covered it with an inverted brandy snifter. He patted Catherine's hand and leaned forward intently.

"Any time, Gilliam."

I relaxed, willing my body and mind into the familiar set. I could feel the force of my mind thrusting palpably against the soft metal of the sinker. I pushed it up the incline until the slopes became slippery steep and my mind was trembling with fatigue. Up ahead the slopes grew steeper still, the altitude more fearful.

"Maybe you shouldn't be trying to push the thing," Warmath said afterward. "You ever try *pulling*?"

"I've tried everything."

"Maybe you just weren't meant to be a telekine," Catherine said with a shake of her head.

"That's what Sandone finally decided."

"No. What I meant was . . . maybe you were meant to be something else. Something *other* than a telekine."

Warmath's head snapped up. "Good thinking, Catty." Turning to me, he asked, "Have you ever tried telepathy, precognition, or any such?"

"No. I was trained to be a telekine."

Warmath rolled the sinker between the ball of his thumb and his forefinger. "Try it again, Gilliam. Only

this time just let yourself follow the most natural course."
He placed the brandy snifter over the sinker again and
sat back.

I shrugged and glanced at the little lead pellet. I
leaned forward and took Catherine's hand. I went into
set.

This time I prowled around the object, viewing it
from all sides, taking my time, letting the force build to
a cresting wave. Tentatively I thrust against the resist-
ing weight, moving it a little way up the incline. Carefully, I herded it along, until the steepness of the slopes
dictated retreat. The unreachable planes of Everest
stretched above, safe valleys beckoned below. I felt
Catherine's hand warm in mine and pushed harder—
and still harder, until my mind screamed for release.

The leaden sinker did not move—it simply and suddenly vanished.

Chapter Four

Below Warmath's mansion was a stream that ran crooked and frost-rimed and aching cold. The wind was brutal above it, whirling sheets of snow and moaning in a thunderous bass monotone as it tuned the high pines.

Inside my heavy parka I watched the snow, my mind casting back to childhood memories of sleds and steaming cider mugs and snow forts.

My mind would not stay in the past, insisting instead upon reliving that moment when the force of Sandone's lens pushed the lead sinker over the top of Everest and into the nothingness beyond.

We did not move for several minutes, simply stared at each other without comprehension. Only later did I realize I could have broken Catherine's hand, so tightly had I squeezed it.

Warmath broke the silence. "Where did it go, Gilliam?"

I shook my head numbly. "I don't know."

"Well, go look. See if you can bring it back."

I gripped Catherine's hand afresh and sank into set. I visualized the little pellet—somewhere—and pulled. There was a resounding *thunk* as something struck the hardwood floor. Warmath reached down and picked it up, holding it between his thumb and forefinger. It was the lead sinker.

Pushing something over the top of Everest proved difficult, and was limited to things of only a few ounces. Bringing the same things back was simplicity itself. It was as if I had pushed a round stone up a hill and balanced it delicately on the rim. Only a nudge was necessary to bring it careening down.

The sculptor vanished for a few moments into his workshop, and then returned with a camera bead, a recorder no larger than a child's marble.

"Here. Teleport this—or whatever it is that you do. We'll see where it goes."

I pushed the bead up the slope, keeping my strength level and my control rigid. At the proper moment, when my brain was quaking with the effort, I took away all restraints and unleashed every quantum of power in me. As it had before, my mind screamed in exquisite pain—and the bead vanished.

I gave the recorder a full minute before pulling it back. It landed with a soft sound against the pillow Warmath had thoughtfully provided.

The little camera's film had been exposed, but revealed nothing but a darkness like that seen in the bottom of a coalsack.

"Hmm—it's not cold, anyway," Warmath mused. "That rules out space, I suppose. Son, you're teleporting these things somewhere, and . . ."

Catherine kissed me. "Juli, let him alone. He's through performing tricks for a while."

"But hell's fire, girl!"

"Shush." She kissed me again and I returned the favor.

While Catherine helped Wanda prepare dinner and Warmath retired somewhat petulantly to his workshop, I shrugged into a heavy parka and wandered through the snow, letting the numbing wind blow against me like a thousand-mile arctic whip.

That evening, fireplace roaring, cognac poured, Warmath tuned to one of the half-dozen news channels.

My eyebrows shot straight up. The man on the television screen was easily recognizable. This time he wore an orange-and-black jumpsuit with "Fannon Ent." emblazoned on the pocket.

Colonel Phillips, I thought wearily. *God*, the man does get around.

He was already in the middle of a press conference, an array of microphones on the podium in front of him, flashbulbs flashing. . . .

He seemed tense, which was understandable under the circumstances.

"Did you know," he was saying, "that at any moment there are as many as fifty wars being fought here on Earth? The causes of those wars pretty much run the gamut. Religious, some of them, with a history going back hundreds—even thousands—of years. Biblical hatreds. Some are caused by an 'unfair' distribution of natural resources." He paused for a moment and then continued. "Maybe a quarter of them are over territory boundaries, boundaries that were changed in *other* wars." He touched his moustache and stared around sadly at the reporters. "Whether for ideological reasons or simply for empire, wars have sapped the Earth's resources and killed countless millions of innocent people.

"Now, at last, we have a technology capable of *stopping* wars. It was developed by Fannon Enterprises under the direction of Avery Fannon himself." He set his jaw grimly, one finger half-raised. "We intend to use that technology, in cooperation with established governments—*or in defiance of them*."

Warmath switched the set off. Face grim, he said,

"We've been getting reports like that all day. In effect, peace by fiat."

"It *could* be a good thing," Catherine said hesitantly. "No wars, a chance for the world to recover . . ."

Warmath shook his head. "No, Cat. It's true we don't have a very good track record for peaceful times, but this is a thousand times worse. Fannon won't be content to remain Up-Top and keep his hands to himself. He's a true sociopath—and he has the world in thrall."

"How can you be sure?" I interjected.

He turned toward me, eyes bleak. "There's a tape I want you to see, Gilliam. I don't think there's another copy in existence. And if Fannon knew I had *this* one . . ." he shook his head without finishing.

Presently, in the castle's huge library, I sat watching what appeared to be a board meeting. Fannon (as usual, black-clad) was one of a dozen sitting around a long oak table.

"This," Warmath said from beside me, "is a special meeting of officers and board members of the failing Colebarth Shipping Company, a minnow that's now part of the Fannon empire. Your father was a major stockholder."

What was laid out (by James M. Colebarth himself) was a plan to save the troubled firm from bankruptcy and stem the hemorrhaging of red ink. When Colebarth was through with the address, he invited comment. Fannon gave it.

"You've gambled a fortune on Colebarth Shipping," Fannon growled. "Because it's an old family business. So what if it is? It's a goddamn dinosaur!"

"Mr. Fannon—"

Fannon barked a laugh. "I could turn Colebarth around in a month—but not with you as part of it. I suggest you resign and let someone who is competent take over. You're an old man. Quit."

Colebarth flushed but held his temper. "How would you 'turn it around,' Mr. Fannon?"

"I'd start by firing three quarters of your personnel," Fannon snapped. "They're a drain on Colebarth Shipping."

"And—?"

Fannon's grin was pure strychnine. "Colebarth Shipping has twenty-four liners. I'd turn them into floating casinos and brothels. That's legal under international law. Minimum investment, maximum return."

Colebarth's face went from red to faintly green. "You're joking!"

"I never joke about business," Fannon returned icily. "I'd rather see the line fold than let you control it."

Fannon stood, his movement lithe, more than ever reminding me of a jungle animal. He snarled at Colebarth, pounded his fist on the table. "What do you think I've been doing the past two weeks? I've been buying up Colebarth stock. Right now I probably own more than you do!"

Now white-faced, Colebarth nonetheless held his ground. "I'll see you in hell, Fannon! The stockholders are loyal to me—to my family!"

"Peterson? Lewison? Pembroke?" Fannon asked jeeringly. "They're pledged to me, now. Your ship is sinking, Colebarth. Get off now—while you can."

"Do you want to force this to a vote, right now?"

"Get wise to yourself," Fannon said ruthlessly. "The Colebarth name is finished."

"Goddamn you!" Colebarth shouted. He appeared dazed. He staggered forward, confronting Fannon. With one hand he grabbed the tycoon's lapel, with the other he slapped Fannon once across the mouth.

It was like igniting a fuse. Fannon's face contorted until it resembled a mask. He stared with burning hatred at Colebarth, his eyes narrowed into slits. Then his fist lashed out, catching the older man beneath the heart.

Savagely, without mercy, Fannon beat the other, pounding his fists into the man's face and midsection. Blood splashed across the table, spattering white shirts.

I studied Fannon's face until the camera went dark. I involuntarily shuddered.

"He'd kill you for what you're thinking right now," Warmath said. He flicked a switch and the lights came up.

"What happened to Colebarth?"

"The man, or the shipping firm?"

"The man."

"He was in the hospital for several months. He's in a sanitarium, now."

"And the shipping firm?"

"Fannon made good on his threat. You may have heard of it—the Good Time Line?"

"No."

Warmath stood up and put his arm around my shoulder. "Funny thing. Even *with* the pledges he'd obtained, Fannon couldn't have done a thing without your father's votes. It was unfortunate for Colebarth that your father died just then. Dean Markham was a sentimental man—probably he'd have voted to keep the line unchanged."

Chapter Five

On our way back to the city I welcomed the electric's dizzying speed and the licking tongue of the wind and snow. Beside me Catherine blinked sleepily at approaching lights and rested her head on my shoulder. We had left Warmath in his castle with promises to advise and inform and drop in whenever.

I flicked on the radio long enough to catch some of the news broadcasts. As long as the emergency lasted, Fannon and those Up-Top would continue to maintain control. In the interests of peace, arsenals around the world were to be reduced and strong sanctions taken against those not in compliance by month's end.

It sounded all very civilized, but I had seen the naked savagery on Fannon's face. I flicked off the radio thinking that a month earlier I would have given my soul to be up there at the Gate.

"Gil?"

"Hmmm?"

"The way you describe what happens when you make things disappear . . . have you ever heard of Sisyphus?"

"He was in Greek legend."

"That's right. A king of Corinth, I think."

"Say on."

"He was punished eternally by having to roll a stone up a mountain. Just when he got it to the top it rolled down again, and he had to start over."

"Um. Maybe he deserved it. He *was* a thief, after all."

She gave me a quick glance. "What's happening to you reminded me of that story."

I said, "What about the people at the bottom of the mountain?"

"What do you mean?"

"They had to watch out for that stone each time it came down."

I dropped Catherine off early (she was teaching a class the next morning) and drove to my own apartment. The city was still in the hush of the storm's passing, the street lights spangles on a string.

Over a glass of Scotch I experimented with my new-found ability. I pushed a small coin up the Everest slopes, then made it reappear behind the butter and mustard in the refrigerator. I dug out a reference book and looked up Sisyphus, just to refresh my memory. Then I had another Scotch and stood in the shower for fifteen minutes, willing the pain in my leg to subside.

Drying off, I considered a coincidence of fact—my father had had an accident just when it was damned convenient for Avery Fannon.

I was considering it more closely when the telephone buzzed.

I jabbed the receive button, expecting to see Catherine's face. Instead, Mark looked back at me. There were circles under his eyes and he had lost weight. He looked exhausted.

"Hello, Gil."

"Hello, Mark. Where in hell are you calling from?"

"Up-Top. I've been trying to get in touch with you for the past two days."

"I was . . . uh, out."

"Yeah. I guess you heard. We put the Babylon Gate into use a few months early."

"I heard," I said.

"It was that, or let Earth blow herself up."

"You don't have to defend your actions to me," I said. "I'm damned happy you were there."

"Thanks. I'm glad you feel that way."

"I do. But the crisis is past, Mark. Ease up a bit."

He smiled ruefully. "I wish we could, Gil. Thing of it is, once we stepped in—made ourselves known—we took the tiger by his tail. Everybody's angry at us. They're calling us every name in the book."

"That never frightened you before."

"It doesn't frighten me now. But I have no desire to spend the rest of my life in prison. That's what will happen if we step down and close the Gate."

"That's nonsense," I said.

"No, it's not," Mark retorted. "Listen to the special UN council tomorrow. We've offended too many people, made too many spear-rattlers lose face."

"Give it a little time, Mark. They'll come around."

He snorted. "Tell me this, Gil. What happens the next time, if the Gate isn't there to stop the bombs?"

"I hear Fannon talking now, Mark. Presumably, we will have learned something from all this."

He grunted disbelievingly. "Well, just in case, we're getting rid of all the missiles."

Something about the way Mark looked prompted me to ask, "Fannon hasn't suggested other steps, has he?"

"Like what?"

"Like moving a few glaciers down to the Sahara, or snuffing out forest fires and widening the Panama Canal. All without asking permission."

Mark shrugged. "He's mentioned a few things. Good things. Gil, we can make Earth a paradise!"

"Maybe so," I said. "But that's not the right way to go about it. Leave it, Mark. Come down—now."

"I can't."

We looked at each other for a moment, and I could see that he was not to be persuaded. Fannon had done his work well. Warmath was right, and I was suddenly scared.

"What does Fannon have on you, Mark? How come he's pulling the strings?"

His mouth compressed, but he didn't say anything.

"You were always an independent cuss," I said. "I don't get it."

"Nothing to get, Gil. Mr. Fannon just happens to be right this time around."

I sighed and said, "What can I do for you, Mark? You must have had some reason to call other than casual debate."

He smiled tightly and ran his fingers through his hair. "It's Alicia," he said. "She's down there on Earth, and we can't locate her. I want you to try to find her."

"Advertise. Move a few clouds around and write yourself a telegram."

"No. You don't understand. If other people know she's not up here, they might try to use her as a weapon. Blackmail."

"Use the Gate to find her."

"We're trying, but there are only four of us, and the world is a big place. There's something else, Gil. She doesn't want to be found. She's avoiding us."

I shrugged. "Then leave her, Mark. She's made her choice. Maybe she can avoid the other people as well."

He shook his head. "We can't do that. We can't take the chance. Besides—I'm in love with her, Gil."

We stared at each other across the megamiles and I finally nodded. "I'll have a try, Mark. Maybe I can come up with something."

He said, "Thanks," shot me another tight smile, and cut the connection.

Sleep would not come. Sometime during the night I realized that I had never gotten around to telling Mark that I could make things vanish—and then reappear. That Sandone had not entirely failed.

Still later, staring at the fugitive shadows that filled the room, I was happy I had not.

In the morning, I thought I knew a way to locate Alicia Fannon.

Chapter Six

Two weeks after I talked to Mark, I got my last visit from the law firm of Spellman, Kurst, Hitchman and Loring.

Their representative was again the youngish attorney who'd introduced himself as Fowler.

He stood politely by the door and asked, "May I come in?"

"Sure." I waved him by. "You caught me at lunch time. Can I get you something?"

"No." He stood and watched me put together a steak and mushroom sandwich. The silence was companionable enough. I took a bottle of wine out of the cupboard, popped the cork, poured myself a glass.

I said, "It's not a bad year—for imitation Neufchateau. You're welcome to join me."

"Perhaps just a little." He held up thumb and forefinger to indicate how much.

I got another glass, poured, and we sat down at a long counter that served me as a table.

He sipped the wine, nodded appreciatively, even smiled a little.

I said, "Red-letter day. S,K,H, and L employ real people. For a while I thought you were all robots."

"Um." It reminded him of his mission. He opened an attaché case, took out a small envelope. "You've completed the requirements set forth by your father. These documents give you legal access to your trust fund. You'll find it's been wisely invested."

I let the envelope lie. My father's money was only of passing interest under the circumstances.

Fowler reached into his case again.

"This is yours, too," he said. "According to his will." He held out a ring bearing a large sapphire.

I turned it around slowly, looking at the spears of light prisming off it. Then I put it in my pocket. "How much is it worth?"

"Enough to buy this apartment building," he said, looking around him. "That, and more."

"Where did my father get it?"

"I don't know."

I finished the sandwich and poured him another glass of Neufchateau.

"Your first name's Baldwin, right?"

He stared at me in surprise. "How did you know that?"

"I looked you up. How is the situation Up-Top affecting Spellman and Group? Is everybody carrying on as usual?"

He looked unhappy. "Yes, sir. What else can we do?"

He had me there. What *could* we do?

I said, "According to my inquiries, you came in second in your class at Georgetown. Attributed to your thoroughness in research. They say you have a brilliant future ahead of you."

He finished his wine and put the glass down.

"How would you like to work for me?"

"You, sir?" He looked at me for five seconds, without

saying another word. Then the smile came back and he nodded.

"Good. I want you to investigate my father's background—particularly where it's linked to Avery Fannon. Start with the Colebarth takeover and go both ways."

He straightened and pulled at his sideburns. "I heard about Colebarth. It's going to take a lot of money."

"Use the trust. All you need." I pushed the envelope toward him.

It was on a weekend, three days before the winter solstice, that I found myself standing beside the fireplace in Catherine's apartment listening to the party's hubbub all around me.

It was a faculty get-together, full of intellectual gossip and discussions—as was usual—on the meaning of Fannon's takeover. For it *was* a takeover, even if President Ralph Dodd still occupied the White House.

Someone—a brunette wearing tortoise-shell glasses— came over with a tray of drinks. I took one and she stayed, putting the tray down on an end table.

She looked at me, said, "Leslie Schouten," and held out her hand.

"Gil Warren."

"You aren't part of the faculty, are you?"

"No. I'm a friend of Catherine's."

"Lucky Catherine." She gave me a smile and a tilt of her head. Across the room Catherine saw us, winked just for me, and then returned to her duties as hostess.

Leslie, it turned out, taught political science. We talked desultorily for several minutes, and then I looked around and saw we'd been joined by another of Catherine's colleagues.

We went through introductions again, and he helped himself to a drink from the tray. His name was Joe Campbell, a tall man of about forty with thinning hair and big shoulders.

They both had opinions about Avery Fannon.

"He hasn't touched the government," Leslie said. "And that's damned smart. It gives the *illusion* that everything's business as usual."

"That's all it is," Campbell replied. "Illusion. And it'll remain illusion only as long as the man in the street isn't affected."

I found myself agreeing. The problem was, though, it *was* affecting the man in the street. There's a kind of glue that holds the fabric of society together—it has to do with knowing where to look for authority. That glue was being loosened, eroded, chipped away.

"Internationally, it's something else," Campbell said with a head shake. "Fannon is moving vast amounts of people from Bangladesh into South Africa. I suppose he thinks he's doing them a kindness. And the governments there have become his puppets."

"Maybe it *will* be a kindness, though," Leslie said with a shrug. "In the long run. He's already destroyed all weapons larger than cannon. *That* can't be all bad."

"But how about that group of protestors in Mexico," Campbell countered. "Fannon killed how many? Twelve? Just by lifting them thirty feet into the air and letting them drop."

I listened to them with half an ear. They talked about absolute power corrupting absolutely. They talked about Fannon moving about the Earth in seven-league boots, working his will. Warmath, I decided, was right. We had climbed into Fannon's frying pan.

Mark called again, and I told him about my arrangements and asked him if it wasn't time he stopped playing God. He had the grace to flush, and his mouth tightened dangerously, but he said nothing.

"That wasn't me in Mexico, Gil," he murmured a few moments later.

"It was *one* of you," I pointed out hotly. "Probably at Fannon's direction."

He just stared at me, his eyes red-rimmed, tired. He had the look of a man on the edge of collapse.

I said then, "Sorry. I should have known you wouldn't have anything to do with that."

"It's okay." And he gave me a ghost of his old smile.

"What's going on up there, anyway? There *were* people not connected with Fannon's Gate."

"They've all been shuttled down," Mark said. "There weren't that many."

"And now Fannon's king of the hill."

His face took on a stubborn look. "You're making a mistake about him, Gil. He's saving the world, not destroying it."

I switched subjects. I wouldn't accomplish anything attacking Fannon directly. I said instead, "You're controlling the government pretty well—right now. You can't watch them all the time, though. They'll find a way to knock Up-Top right out of the sky."

"No, they won't." Mark grinned a little, shifted in his chair. "All rockets, shuttles, and other craft capable of reaching orbit are being moved to Denver Center. No one's going to threaten us. And don't forget, we've got a computerized army—and Fanny Six."

"You can't control what you don't see," I pointed out. "There'll be an underground, and they'll probably be building a hidden rocket."

"Several undergrounds have *already* formed," he said musingly. "We're watching them. When the time is ripe we'll deal with them." He shot me a glance. "No one knows what our power is *really* like."

"Mark—"

Without saying anything else, he disconnected.

I received a note two days later from Baldwin Foster. I burned it, put on my coat, and tramped through

foot-deep snow to a bar off Turner Road. He was waiting in the last booth, his features lost in shadow.

"Beer?"

"Why not? You're paying for it."

I sat, waited until the beer arrived, and then looked
at him inquiringly.

"I've spent a lot of your money," he said. "Went
through old records, looked up people everybody thought
were dead. There's a picture that's emerging."

"Give me the picture."

He took a swallow of beer. "You've studied languages.
Do you know the Greek word *boulimia*?"

"Insatiable appetite."

"That's right. Fannon is the living definition of that
word." He paused long enough to light up a scented
cigarette. "A robber-baron like Morgan or Gould wouldn't
have lasted three minutes with Fannon. Your father
and he crossed paths maybe half a dozen times, and
each time your father lost."

I gripped my glass of beer. "Did Fannon kill him?"

"Maybe. It's likely." Fowler's face twisted in disgust.
"You'll never prove it."

In New York City a narcotics dealer named Ralphie
Stimson was found impaled on the spire of the East
River Trade Center, otherwise known as the Giant
Needle.

Vice-President Frederick Brubaker gave a speech before 2,000 members of the Maryland Maritime Union.
He praised Avery Fannon's "cooperative efforts" and
pledged to support him wherever possible. He looked
pasty-faced.

A family of self-styled "wilderness rebels" was wiped
out by a tornado as they were crossing Lone Creek in
upstate Maine.

Two hundred fanatical muslim guerillas were killed

trying to storm the U.S. embassy in Baghdad. Survivors said their friends were crushed by the "hand of Satan."

Business as usual.

Winter deepened, and the winds sliced through me like ragged knives. Given the opportunity, I will always make summer my choice. Winter is for masochists and martyrs.

One evening, when light still glimmered slate-gray in the west, I received a visit from Fannon. His way—and it had me swearing off alcohol for a month.

I was in my apartment, contemplating Rembrandt. Beyond the french windows the wind was pounding and shuffling. Lately my leg had begun to ache again, reminding me of nights in Africa, hunkering in the mud as cannon rounds came over.

There was a knock on the door.

Glad of the interruption, I got to my feet and swung the door open. Fannon walked in. Or at least a wild, ragged doppleganger of him.

He moved without sound, floating approximately six inches off the floor. He was constructed of pieces of cloth and air and what seemed like chalk dust. His hair was a storm of fur and dust. Sometimes I could see through him—in the interstices of neck and jaw, in the creases where wrists joined hands.

But it was indisputably Fannon. I stepped back in shock, and the Fannon-thing drifted by me, settling finally in a chair without denting the cushion. There was a high-pitched, vibrating sound, as though the air itself was alive.

"Sit down, Gilliam," the Fannon-thing said. The voice was hollow, appropriately vague.

I sat, and we stared at each other. Fannon grinned, showing a flannel tongue and the ghosts of teeth.

"This—body—is courtesy of the Babylon Gate. Chester is controlling the simulacrum."

I'd recovered a little, and forced a shrug. "Very impressive. What can I do for you, Mr. Fannon?"

"As Chester told you, Gil, there are underground forces operating here on Earth. We know most of them—it's the ones we *don't* know about that worry us."

I grimaced and studied the simulacrum afresh. Mark sometimes allowed an arm to dissolve, joining the bulky stir of the creature's body. I could imagine him, the flesh taut across his cheekbones, eyes glimmering with effort, the wires from his head running off into the Babylon Gate.

I said, "Is this how you talked to the heads of government?"

"It seems to be effective."

"I'll bet. No *wonder* you can control them. You're the ultimate bogeyman."

"We were talking about the underground," he prompted after a moment.

"You're going to have to expect resistance," I told Fannon. "You've chosen to play God. There will be people who won't live that way."

The Fannon-thing smiled again, coldly, the chips of eyes strangely alive. "Do you include yourself in that number, Gil?"

"Are you here to determine my loyalties?"

"No. Only to revise your timetable. It is known that Alicia is not with us. As a result, she is in deadly danger."

"Have you ever wondered why she's hiding from you, Fannon?"

"What do you mean?"

"She might not like what you've become."

The Fannon-thing looked long at me, and I felt the chill. "Careful, Gilliam."

I shrugged. "I promised Mark I would look for her. I'll do that."

"And hurry," Fannon snapped. Abruptly he was gone,

and the thing took on Mark's aspect. The body loomed larger, more substantial.

"You've made him angry, Gil. It's a good thing you're my brother."

"Stop this thing, Mark. Kick that crazy man out and come down, before he makes you a monster, too."

The thing hesitated. Its features twisted in anguish. "I can't, Gil," it said.

"Why the hell not?"

There was no answer. It took a step toward me and began to dissolve, falling with a muffled clatter on the floor.

That night I made a decision. To save Mark—to save myself—I would have to kill Avery Fannon.

I lingered long. I considered the possibilities.

Chapter Seven

Came a night in the month named for the two-faced God.

Came Warmath and Warren *en prise*.

What can you say when Julius Warmath throws a wingding? It was held in the museum, and marked the occasion of Warmath's second contribution to that august institution. Everyone expected him to top his previous performance. They weren't disappointed.

I entered the museum via a silver sliding board. Two girls dressed as matadors caught me deftly, stood me up, dusted me off, set me on a slidewalk that wended its way through a gallery of bending lights. At the bottom of a rainbow of smokey orange and vibrant blue an oriental slave-girl emerged coquettishly from a golden lamp. She bid me welcome.

I joined the guests at play.

Here and there among us stalked holographic lions, so real their piano teeth and strident roars made our marrows chill. I glanced around, saw Catherine, sent a smile, received one, and turned away to scan the crowd. I figured if Alicia would show up for anything, it would be for another Warmath extravaganza.

I got a drink and sipped it, easing myself between two shrieking harpies. I paused to look at Chiron, his brazen glory overshadowed for the moment. Slipping beneath the protecting rope, I ran my fingers over the shaggy explosion of mane, down the ridged planes of his neck. I looked into the cups of his eyes.

It began to rain in the museum, glittering drops of tinsel, long streamers of gold thread. I stopped a waiter, got a new drink, and wandered, jockeying through the ebb and flow of bodies, my mind immune to the screech of voices—immune because I had murder on my mind.

Eventually the house lights dimmed. A chorus of voices sang *hallelujah*. A single blue spotlight fell on a holographed whirlwind that sped to and fro among the guests like an airborne Puck. The whirlwind dissolved and was Warmath, a cherubic grin stretched across his face. He made a leg and winked.

At that moment I saw Alicia Fannon. She was sipping an iced drink along one wall. She was disguised, her hair blonde, her height accentuated by four-inch heels. It wasn't that bad a disguise, if I hadn't known she would be there.

Casually, I edged my way toward her.

Warmath had grabbed a microphone, and his voice filtered through the crowd from a hundred hidden speakers.

"Dear me! Oh, dear *me*! I feel I *must* tell you—one of these lions is real!"

There was a collective gasp, and scattered nervous applause. Then there were one or two screams as the lions prowled too close for some to bear. Amid the hubbub two more guests made a late appearance. The man dressed in black glanced my way and gave a cold smile. The big blond man noticed me and nodded.

On the stage Warmath snapped his fingers. Velvet drapes were lifted off his newest work of art. Poised forever in brass, eternal as Aphrodite, Catherine looked

down upon her subjects. Warmath had caught the heart
of her, and molded it in metal. A lump formed in my
throat. It *was* Catherine. Chiron, I thought, you lucky
bastard! You'll never be lonely again.

Then, slowly, I turned away from the stage. I pointed
my finger to where Alicia was standing. Mark nodded,
Fannon did not.

Warmath completed his performance. At another snap
of his fingers, a huge black-maned lion jumped up on
the stage. Smiling happily, the artist swung himself
aboard. Without a backward glance, man and lion exited.
House lights flickered on and applause swelled.

Suddenly everyone was aware that the show had
changed settings. Heads swiveled and there were gasps
as Fannon was recognized.

They moved through the crowd easily, not worried
about assassination attempts. Why should they be? Their
protection was absolute. Anyone who approached nearer
than ten feet was brushed back by a massive and none-
too-gentle hand. They were regal, impervious, and arrogant; nothing could harm them.

Except a teleport.

Alicia saw them and tried to run. She stumbled on
her stiletto heels, tore them off, slipped under the rope
separating the throng from the museum's exhibits. She
disappeared among glass display cases.

"Get her!" Fannon cried. He ran forward a few steps
and stopped, peering into the darkness beyond.

Mark circled Chiron's giant form, then glanced upward, where a fleeting Alicia briefly appeared on the
gallery stairs.

"Alicia!" His head and shoulders were momentarily
caught in the blue spot. Seemingly without effort, he
rose into the air. Gasps came from the audience. Though
it was common in rumor, few had actually seen telekinesis.

At the top of the mezzanine railing he stopped, grasping a wooden balustrade for balance, staring down the curving stair. Alicia saw him and stopped, chest heaving.

"Get out of my way!" she screamed at him. She came straight for him, fingers extended into claws.

I watched the drama with half an eye, intent upon Fannon, who stood with head thrown back and hands resting on hips. Everyone, like Fannon, was looking up. I wouldn't get an opportunity like this again. I went into set—and let a micro-grenade slide down the Everest slopes and materialize on the floor in front of him.

He saw it, and a look of disbelief flickered over his face. Then the explosion hurled him against the museum wall, blood spurting from nose and mouth, the front of his skull smashed beyond recognition.

"No, Jesus! No!" Mark was staring over the railing, his face horror-stricken, Alicia struggling in his grasp. Abruptly he shook with a galvanic spasm, his arms flailing. Alicia pushed against him, raking her nails across his face. He fell against the rail, jerking spasmodically, reaching as though for Fannon. And then he went over. This time telekinesis did not slow his fall.

"Mark! For the love of God!" I made my way toward him. Something was *wrong, wrong*! What had happened? At the same time, a leaden feeling formed in my stomach.

I leaned over, took his hand, felt for a pulse. There was none; his neck was twisted at an unnatural angle.

The crowd was running in every direction, panic taking over locomotor centers. I was unaware of them. I felt cold, numb. I had willingly committed regicide, but I had not intended fratricide. I had not! I clenched Mark's hand and tasted the blurring salt of tears.

Kneeling there, something flashed across my mind—a reference to the master-thief Sisyphus, so noted for his cleverness. It was said he slew travelers who would be his friends, that he revealed the hiding places of fugitive women. I knew now what happened at the bottom of that mountain when the rock came crashing down.

Sisyphus!

Ah, Sisyphus!

For this your punishment awaits.

Chapter Eight

We have three Gods. Three unknown and terrible Gods.

They live Up-Top, perigee 21,180 miles, apogee 22,652 miles. Nothing on Earth is beyond their reach.

They can pull down buildings, walk uninhibited through walls of brick and steel. They're invisible when they want to be, vengeful when they choose to be, wrathful when their wish is thwarted.

Right now they were hunting me.

It was two days since I'd killed Fannon, since the surreal events that snuffed out Mark's life. And I still wasn't able to assimilate it. *Why* had Mark fallen? *How* had he lost control? True, Alicia had pushed him. Still—

I stood just inside the window of the roach-haven I'd rented and stared out at the three-quarter moon. My left leg hurt where the metal fragments had torn and scarred the tissue. It was bearable—nothing to the hurt I felt inside through the tears and scars of *that* tissue.

In the turmoil following the explosion and Mark's fall, I had mingled with the crowd, taking advantage of the confusion. At the first opportunity I bolted, picking an exit that led into an alley behind the museum. I ran.

Sooner or later, I knew, the remaining telekines would figure out I was the one they wanted. It wouldn't be too difficult; everyone knew I had arranged Warmath's showing. Only I had known Fannon would be there—and finally, Mark had trusted me.

I changed my hair from black to brown, accentuated my cheekbones, flattened my nose. I wore blue contact lenses. To the casual observer, I didn't look like Gilliam Warren, double-murderer.

Outside, a cloud obscured the moon. It glowed faintly, softly, with a nimbus of stolen light. I watched until the moon broke free again, a baleful eye in the heavens. Then I turned away and sat down on the filthy bed. After a while I got up, poured myself a tumbler full of cheap whiskey, and turned on the antique television set that occupied one corner of the room.

At a newsbreak, they showed more pictures of the museum, with chalk-marked lines where the bodies had been recovered. They interviewed several of the guests. They showed pictures of me in my army days and later ones, when I was in training with Sandone. I would be found, the gods said, or reprisals would be taken.

Gil Warren—the most wanted man on Earth.

If Mark had lived, of course, the whole thing might well have been over. Fannon had corrupted him—how, I didn't know—but he was still reachable, still the Mark I knew. With him gone the cards had fallen, all been scattered. All that remained now were three kings— and a fugitive joker.

I thought about Warmath and Catherine. It was likely I'd never see either of them again. To go anywhere near them was to invite capture. I remembered the bronze nude in the museum and was reminded of something Warmath had told me but not made public. The sculpture of Catherine, like *Centaur*, was kinetic. If I got lonely enough, I could always go back to the museum.

I turned off the television set and drew myself a bath

of rusty hot water. As I let myself down into the tub, I found myself thinking about the three remaining telekines. I had seen them, but too briefly to remember much. One was large, bearded; one was young. The other man had been thin, average-looking. Beyond that, they were mysteries.

Sandone had worked on his Phase State subjects serially, with me last and Mark next to last. Based upon that small amount of evidence, it appeared Sandone had put more and more effort in his final subjects. Mark had been given thirty-six sessions, I had had forty-four. The three remaining telekines would probably possess less telekinetic ability than Mark.

I shivered. It didn't really matter, the Gate made them giants.

The hot water eased the ache in my leg, and I lay there until I began to feel sleepy. Outside I could hear the winding-down sounds of the city—the blare of horns and the occasional far-off *hee-haw* of police sirens.

The government, reluctantly, was still cooperating with the remaining three Up-Top. I supposed that if there were a way to reach them, to negate their power, the story might be very different. Until that time, however, there was little choice.

I wondered if all the world's leaders had had a ghostly visit. Chances were they had.

After soaking for twenty minutes I felt better. I climbed out of the tub, wrapped myself in one of the thin towels provided by the hotel, and padded across the room to the window. The moon was hidden again, gleaming only faintly behind massed dark clouds.

Being free wouldn't last forever, I knew. I needed a plan.

It was early in the morning of the third day. I had gotten some sleep, but I felt far from rested. Half the night I had tossed in the grip of nightmares. The other half I had spent pacing, thinking.

A little after seven I dressed and took the creaky elevator to the ground floor. I looked out on the day. No policemen came to arrest me, no invisible hands grabbed me.

The air was cold, filled with fine particles. I turned up my coat collar and slitted my eyes. Like scores of other pedestrians, I walked briskly along the avenues. I wondered if the gods were watching.

I had breakfast at a hash-house that catered to the derelict trade, finding a table by itself that faced the entrance. I ignored the sour odors, ordered toast and coffee, and watched the others eat. Over a second cup of coffee I read a paper some other patron had left behind.

The Gods had named themselves—*trium virorum*—The Triumvirate.

The building that housed Sandone's laboratory was indistinguishable from the several surrounding it. It had a front formed of glass and stone. Concrete steps led to recessed doorways. Function had been this architect's handmaiden, not aesthetics.

I stopped on the sidewalk and hunched my shoulders against the cutting knives of the wind. A police car turned left and passed by slowly, its occupants methodically checking the crowd. Heart pounding, mouth dry, I watched them gain the next intersection and turn off. For the present, at any rate, my disguise seemed to be working.

Still apprehensive, I climbed the steps, pushed through one of the recessed doors, and followed the familiar corridors around to the laboratory wing.

It was dark there. The green tiled room was illuminated only by a small amount of light that seeped through a glass door farther down the corridor.

Sandone's office was bare, stripped even of furniture. I left it, moved out into the laboratory again, slumped down in one of the sculptured chairs. Glass surfaces reflected my new face back at me mockingly. A stranger's face, lonely, frightened.

The lighted door down the corridor revealed a narrow office, a battered steel desk with a time clock on it. A guard sat behind it, his feet propped up, his chair tipped back against the wall. He was an old man, worn out with living. A rime of white stubble covered the lower half of his face.

I knocked to get his attention, leaned in.

"I'm looking for Dr. Sandone," I said. "Know where I can find him?"

The old man took his time. He sat up and adjusted his uniform cap, wiped ineffectually at the coarse stubble. He peered at me suspiciously for several seconds.

"Who are you?"

I gave him the name I'd used on the hotel register. "John Shaw."

"I haven't seen you here before."

I shrugged. "How long have you been working here?"

"Since they closed the wing. Three months or so."

"That must be why. I met Sandone about a year ago."

The old man stared at me closely for a moment longer, then seemed to arrive at a decision. He put both hands flat on the desk surface and stood up.

"Dr. Sandone's Up-Top," he said. "With *Them*."

I stared. "Up-Top? With the . . . Triumvirate?" My heart sank.

He nodded, then looked at me with a small spark of interest.

"Why do you want to know?"

"I owe him something," I said with some truth. I started to turn away. Sandone had been my last chance. Through him I had intended to find out (at the very least) more about the Triumvirate. It hadn't occurred to me he would be on the Platform with them.

I turned back abruptly. "There was someone else here," I said. "A technician who worked with Sandone. His name was Toby Roberson. You know where *he* is?"

"It important?"

I nodded. "Could be."

"That's too bad," the old man said ruminantly. "I heard he went off and joined a cult." He picked up his time clock and hung it over his shoulder.

"Oh? What cult?"

The guard shook his head. "He had to be crazy, if you ask me. They call themselves Deathclockers. Live on an island off the coast of Mexico somewhere." He shook his head again. "Crazy."

The Ohio River had the dull color of lead. Near midday, the wind grew in force, whipping the sullen water into whitecaps. It moaned sonorously beneath the bridges.

I grabbed a sandwich and a cup of coffee at a down-at-the-heels restaurant and headed back toward my hotel room. I wanted another hot bath—my leg hurt.

A block from the hotel, the Gods descended.

By itself, the swirling snow and surging wind gave an illusion of other-worldliness. Now, as if to complete the illusion, a man on the other side of the street began to climb eerily into the sky. His feet thrashed, his face revealed shock.

I stood and watched. I was both terrified and fascinated.

As far as I could see, the man's only crime was to have dark hair and my approximate height and build. He struggled futilely in an invisible massive grip, twisting and scrabbling, his frightened cries muted by the wind. Fingers the size of fence-posts plucked at his trousers, stripping them away. He was held rigid while the Gods examined his legs. It wasn't difficult to deduce what they sought. Shrapnel wounds. Finding none, the man was discarded with a casual disdain. He fell the twenty feet or so to the concrete below, landing heavily on his back and shoulders.

Letting out a long breath, I turned left at the first corner I came to. The incident had occurred too close to my hotel to be a coincidence; I couldn't go back there.

I walked, keeping my stride brisk but unhurried. Police were everywhere, and above, invisibly, the Gods. The sooner I left the city, the better.

The remainder of the afternoon I spent in a little bar not far from the Ohio River. When nightfall came I stepped outside, turned south, and walked.

Ten miles farther on I crossed railroad tracks. In time-honored fashion I hopped a slow freight going westward. It was a cold night and I was tired. I rubbed my leg to ease the ache and sipped sparingly from the bottle of Scotch I'd bought earlier. Through cracks in the doorway I caught glimpses of the moon. A good sign; it meant the storm was passing. Sometime later, lulled by the monotonous rumble of the rails, I curled up beside a bale of straw. Slowly, imperceptibly, I fell asleep.

Chapter Nine

When I was ten, I ran away from home. "Home" was a hard-scrabble farm on a creek outside Topeka, Kansas. My foster father caught up with me, dragged me back, and beat me. That night he locked me up in the root cellar.

"You're staying there until you learn not to run," he called to me through the door planking.

I smelled the earth, the dry pungent odor of burlap. The blackness was total. It was cold, too, and I started to cry.

"Won't do any good—I aim to teach you a lesson." He pushed the bolt in angrily, then strode off toward the stairs.

His name was Jake Corsorian, a wild-haired powerful man who took me in for the welfare money. His wife, a timid soul with cataracts in both eyes, deferred totally to his wishes.

There had been, I supposed, other children taken in by the Corsorians. Where they were now was open to question. Grown up and gone, probably—the only certain way to beat Jake.

The cellar was ten feet square. I prowled its perimeter, hands groping, mouth open, sucking at the stale air. In one corner my fingers touched a slight depression, a place where the earth was softer than elsewhere. Buried there, I found the stub of a candle, a box of kitchen matches. Some other child had been interred here, too!

Jake kept me in the cellar three days, and when I got out I ran away again.

I dreamed of Jake and the Gods as I rolled westward on the freight train, then woke up and had another sip from the bottle of Scotch. I rose from beside the bale of straw, opened the door a crack, peered out at the red-streaked dawn. The air was cold, fresh, hinting of moisture and new snow. It occurred to me that I might have traded Jake Corsorian for something far worse. As bad as he had been, he was at least knowable, and in his way, consistent.

I changed trains several times, going randomly west and south. Most of the empty freights were closed and locked, but a few cars—older stock mostly—allowed entry.

It was getting appreciably warmer. No more fires in tin plates to ward off the cold. Now I dozed, half wrapped in a railroad man's discarded overcoat, while the rails sang their song beneath me.

Alex Metcalf once told me about a place—a ghost town—near Bigfoot, Texas. People could disappear there, he said. It was somewhere between San Antonio and Mexico. A good place to go if you didn't want to answer questions, if you needed time to think.

The Triumvirate was still searching for me in Pittsburgh, turning the city upside down. The city/state/federal government was helpless, of course, though the official line was still "mutual cooperation to curb lawlessness."

*   *   *

Pueblo Suerte was a cluster of time-weathered buildings baking in the sun. Half a mile away was an abandoned mine. The *town of luck* had had no luck at all; it
was now a hobo camp.

The first man I met was wearing faded pajamas and
two weeks' worth of whiskers. He stared at me for a
moment and then grinned. "I expect you're hungry."

"And thirsty," I said.

"Got any money?"

"Not much."

"Go to the last building on the left," he pointed with
a skinny finger. "Ask for Panama. He'll feed you first
time on the house. After that you got to work for it."

I did as he suggested. The meal was a mongrel off-
shoot of chili, hot and satisfying. Panama turned out to
be Sam Portner, an ex-circus clown who had grown
weary of two o'clock matinees. He remembered Alex.
He was a genial little man, gray-haired, blue-eyed,
wiry. He didn't ask questions; that wasn't the way in
Pueblo Suerte.

I slept inside the mine, rolled up in a borrowed
blanket.

The population of the pueblo varied from week to
week. It was a crossroads, a way station for derelict
souls. There were thieves, students, artists, freaks, and
misfits of all sorts. Alex had been right; a man could
disappear in Pueblo Suerte.

Sam Portner was the only constant. He healed the
sick, fed the hungry, settled disputes—with a double-
barreled shotgun in his hand—and, sometimes, buried
the dead. Once a week he drove into San Antonio for
supplies and medicine. For a fat percentage and no
questions asked, he fenced stolen goods to an underworld contact.

Looking benign and cool, Sam sat on his shaded
porch, staring out at the rim of cliffs ten miles away.

"Up in San Antone I saw pictures of this fellow Gil

Warren," he murmured, sipping at a half-empty bottle of beer. "He's wanted pretty bad. A two-time killer. I'm surprised he made it out of Pittsburgh."

I glanced at him, but his eyes did not stray from the cliffs. I said hesitantly, "Maybe he's still there."

"Um." Sam shook his head, up-ended his beer. When he was through, he sighed gustily, said softly, "Why don't you come see me tonight. In the back room of the store—about midnight."

The moon rose that evening, three-quarters full, the cliffs beneath it matte-black, shadow-etched. I gathered my belongings, rolled them into the blanket, tossed it over my shoulder. I might be leaving in a hurry.

Sam's back room was a surprise. He had a library, an up-to-date computer, and a stock of vintage whiskies. He waved me in, smiling, indicating the floor for my rolled duffle, a leather armchair for me.

"Care for a drink?"

"No," I said.

He grinned and nodded.

"What is this about?"

Bluntly, he said, "It's about that . . . Tri-umvirate, or whatever they call themselves. They're hunting you."

I felt ice in my stomach. "My name's John Shaw."

"Sure it is." He sat in a chair that was a twin to mine. Delicately, he lit a cigar. "Most people don't know how to disguise themselves," he remarked conversationally. "They always leave something out. Eyes, lips, ears—something. If you're in the business of looking, you can generally spot it."

I thought of Alicia Fannon. She had disguised herself and I had seen through it easily, because I knew what I was looking for. Maybe Sam had something.

I shrugged. "What did I do wrong?"

"Not so much wrong, just not enough right." He exhaled a plume of blue smoke. "Your height hasn't changed. The hair is the same—just another color. And your accent is as distinctive as a fingerprint." He looked at me. "You've been lucky, so far. It won't last forever."

"How do you know so much?"

He shrugged. "It was what I did for a living, not so long ago."

"A clown?" I asked derisively.

"That's right. Thirty years in the business. Gawdy-Gawdy the Clown, they called me." He gave me a hard glance. "You don't have to sneer at that; I was the best quick-change artist on the circuit. I learned things—" He stopped, scratched his head, rolled the cigar between his thumb and fingers. After a moment, he said quietly, "Point is, you won't make it without help. Them Gods are gonna find you."

With my fingertip, I traced the grain in the chair's polished leather. Then I studied Sam's face for five or six seconds. He didn't blink.

"Is it going to cost much, this help?"

"How much have you got?"

I put my hand in my pocket, pulled out the sapphire ring. "No money. But maybe you can find somebody who would buy this."

He took it, turned it over slowly in his hands. He twisted his mouth. "This looks valuable enough, but it'll be hard to place. I'll try next trip up to San Antone." He smiled, and I found myself smiling in return.

"Now how about that drink?"

"You have Scotch?"

"Sure. Around here someplace."

Afterwards, I lay awake for a long while, thinking of the Babylon Gate, moonlit deserts, mad men, dead men, centaurs, and all the legends of Sisyphus. *Chainer of death . . . master of confusion . . . even Hell itself failed to hold him.* I followed that skein of thought until the world grew heavy and the stars dimmed, then let the darkness draw me in, enfold me.

*   *   *

The second week after my meeting with Sam he drove to San Antonio a day early. When he returned he presented me with an oil-cloth pouch, wallet-sized. It bulged with notes of all denominations.

He shrugged his shoulders, said, "You been had. They gave less than a quarter of what that ring was worth."

I tucked the pouch in place beneath my belt. "Never mind, Sam. I want to go with you next time—to the city."

"Why? You're only inviting trouble for yourself."

"I know," I said. "But still—"

He gave me a look. "Then you'd better let me teach you a few things about disguises."

"You'll find me a willing enough pupil."

He snorted, then laughed and clapped me on the back. "And you'll find *me* a damned expensive teacher."

The library in San Antonio overlooked the canal. I walked up two dozen steps, stepped through the revolving door. It was a bright day, already hot at ten A.M.; the blasts of air conditioning inside the building quickly began the process of freeze-drying me. As best I could I ignored it. On the fourth floor I found the section on religions.

The experience of epiphany, I suppose, can overtake a person at any time. Scanning down the lists of healers, gurus, self-styled prophets, mystics, and evangelists, I was struck by a bolt of foolish cynicism. I dug further into the stacks, came away with what I sought.

The Deathclockers were not a charismatic organization, at least not in the same sense of being divinely inspired. Rather, they were religious mutineers, misfits, rebels thumbing their noses at convention. Their patron saint, if they'd claimed one, would likely have roared around on a Harley Davidson.

The cult was founded by one Max Wilson, a physicist who'd camped at Trinity Site, illegally, for five months. *His* epiphany was one of despair, borne of micro-rads and fused aluminum silicates.

I am a time-binder, he'd told his followers. *With seconds of diamonds, and minutes of gold*.

For a year he walked the land, and then abruptly, with his flock, he'd vanished.

He left a mailing address, though, and I wrote it down on the back of an old envelope.

"They have wonderful silicones and adhesives these days," Panama Sam told me six days later. "With a couple of tubes in your pocket you can be just about anybody you choose." He squeezed some silicone onto his hand, applied it lightly, teased it, as a sculptor teases clay. His nose grew half an inch longer, the bridge higher. He looked into the pocket mirror he'd put on the table, did something to his eyes, popped a plastic bridge into his mouth. Closing his eyes tightly, he sprayed himself with holding agent.

"Well?" he asked.

Panama Sam was a different man. Older, with mushed-in cheeks and faintly bucked teeth. He stood up, slowly, arthritically, and shambled toward me.

Beginning to end, it had taken maybe thirty seconds.

I said, "Wonderful!" and meant it.

"Most of it's simple misdirection," he muttered, turning back to the table. "Visual sleight of hand."

"I could never learn to do that."

"If you learn just a few tricks it should see you through," was his comment. He studied me in the mirror. "You heard from them Deathclock people?"

I shook my head.

"My guess you won't. That sort like to be left alone."

When he was himself again he stored the tubes in the grouch sack he wore around his neck. Then he opened the refrigerator and took out a couple of beers. We talked about the Triumvirate and the world at large and watched the sun disappear behind the rim of cliffs.

"They going to destroy all government, take it over all by themselves?" Sam took a long swallow.

I said, "They have the high ground right now. And Fanny Six. They can pretty much do what they want. Who's going to stop them?"

"You, maybe?"

I snorted, but my heart wasn't in it. If *not* me, then indeed who? I told him, "Probably they'll leave the governments in place. Most of them, anyhow. That much less for them to run. I don't think they want chaos. Not just now, anyway."

"You know them?"

"I've seen them. They didn't *look* dangerous. But neither does a coral snake."

He said sourly, "News is being controlled. The copy out of Washington and New York is so much pablum."

We finished our beers and opened two more. Out in the desert there was a cry of a night bird.

"Owl," Sam said, giving me a glance. "Been out there ever since I opened this place. Good at his work."

The following morning Sam climbed into his truck and swung it around so that its nose pointed north. It was Thursday, his day to go into San Antonio.

I walked down from the mine, opened the far door, said, "Got room for a passenger?"

He stared at me. My nose was a misshapen lump, my hair greased back and tied by a string. I'd restructured my eyebrows and added half an inch to my jawline. When I walked, I used an Igor-like limp.

"Gawd-a-mighty!" He grinned his delight. "How long did you work on that?"

"An hour, more or less."

"Well, no one would think you're John Shaw. I suppose it'll do." He laughed out loud and motioned me in.

*   *   *

Sam was silent for a time as he shifted gears and steered around the switchbacks leading to the highway. Then he said, "You're going to go see those Clockers, aren't you?"

"I had it in mind," I said.

"Thought so. You *could* stay on at the pueblo. I could use a second-in-command." He looked at me pensively.

"Thanks." I gave him a grin to show my appreciation, then shook my head. "I have to see a man there."

"Might be more trouble than you figured for. Those Deathclockers sound strange—even for these times."

"Yeah," I acknowledged, "they do. And it might be. But I've still got to go."

He dropped me at the edge of town and I took a bus, then a taxi. I spent some of the ring money on things both expensive and illegal. I evoked Sam's name, and they showed me courtesy and deference.

When my purchasing was done, I wandered for a time by the underground canal and had coffee at a sidewalk cafe. I people-watched. And after a while I bought a newspaper and skimmed through it.

The Triumvirate, it seemed, were all over the world, doing good and spreading harmony. That's if you didn't read between the lines. If you did, then you got a choked feeling like a bone might be stuck in your throat.

At five o'clock I reversed my route with taxi and bus. When I disembarked, I could see Sam's truck two blocks down the street.

Unhurriedly, I limped-strolled up a side-street, then crossed over and headed for a corner grocery store.

All the time I was walking, I was cursing, thinking—*damn! damn!*—somewhere I'd made a mistake. Sam's parking the truck two blocks away was a signal. It meant the Gods had tracked me here to San Antonio. It meant I was to get away—and *not* try to help Sam.

I eyed the shelves of canned peas, selected two jars of dill pickles, passed by the pureed baby food. All the while I considered. It was possible the Triumvirate knew about the sapphire ring, had feelers out to fences all over the country. They'd only had to wait. And Sam, of course, was the one caught in their net.

I paid for my purchases, exited the store, limped off toward a development of medium-priced stucco houses.

Were they watching me? What would they do with Sam?

The bright sun beat down, tarnished now, on the world.

Goddamn it, Sam! Goddamn it!

Chapter Ten

I went aboard the skimmer in a rush, my duffle bag dangling over one shoulder. I took a seat on the deck, somberly aware I was the only passenger.

As I watched, a heavyset man climbed down from the bridge, looked at me through jaded eyes, and disappeared through an open hatch. Glancing around, I caught surreptitious stares from half a dozen crewmen. I found myself grinning sourly. It figured; they were curious. After all, who but a Deathclocker would book passage to Clock Island?

A tall man in pressed whites approached. He stopped a few feet away and studied me.

"My name is Marsh," he said. "I'm captain here. The passenger list says you're outbound for the Clocker camp."

I manhandled my deckchair into a more comfortable position before answering, then let my duffle bag slide to the deck beside me. I rested my hand on it.

"That's what my ticket says. The skimmer goes there, doesn't it?"

Marsh nodded. "Just wanted to make sure you know what you're getting into."

"Thanks," I said. "I know."

There was a deep-throated roar below, and the skimmer suddenly began to vibrate. Marsh touched his cap and moved away. A moment later the craft turned its bows to the open sea and the muffled roar became a banshee scream. With a lurch, the skimmer began to move.

At better than forty knots, we would reach the Clocker enclave in under an hour. I opened the duffle bag far enough to find a battered safari hat. Drawing it down over my eyes, I leaned back in my deck chair and attempted to get some sleep. I might need it later on.

Briefly, I thought of Sam Portner. Although it took some doing, I had found his obituary in one of the small community papers. Death, it said, was by natural causes.

And I have a bridge to sell to anyone who'd believe that.

"There's the island," Captain Marsh said some time later. He pointed to a hump of gray and green that jutted out of the ocean like a giant's elbow. The skimmer swung about, cut its speed, and began an approach.

I gathered up my belongings. At first glance the island appeared normal, even a trifle dreary—just your average small tropical island.

The skimmer nibbled its way onto a beach of rusty-looking sand and three crewmen began unloading boxes onto a raised wooden platform.

"Been making these runs for four years," Marsh said from behind me. "Bringing in supplies. Almost never see any Clockers."

"How do they pay for it?"

"We get a check," Marsh replied. "It comes from a mainland account." He shrugged a little, and placed both hands on the railing.

"Well, thanks," I said. I threw my duffle bag over the side, then followed it immediately by vaulting over the rail. I waved to Marsh, picked up the bag, walked inland without a backward glance.

It was an unremarkable island. About two miles long by one wide, it was covered with scrub brush and a few strands of twisted cypress. The highest point was a rocky promontory that brooded over a narrow lagoon.

I was aware of being watched. Not by Gods, this time. I caught a flicker of movement from the corner of my eyes and ignored it. There was a trail leading up from the beach and I followed that, stopping only when I came to a fork.

There were two Clockers there, sitting on a stump.

I put the duffle bag down. "I'm Corry Hillman," I said. "I sent word that I was coming."

They studied me in silence for a while, then they stood up, one on either side. The one to my left was well over six feet, his knuckles crisscrossed with scars. The smaller one looked rock-solid. He grinned at me. Their death-clocks, prominent above their left eyebrows, gleamed white and hard.

I stepped back and turned my body slightly, keeping both men in view.

"Uh, look," I said. "Maybe we ought to go see Max Wilson. He's the one I wrote to."

The smaller man began to talk in tongues.

The big man curled his fists into bludgeons, a certain joyful spark lighting up his eyes.

Too late, I heard the sound of footsteps behind me. I spun around, my right fist whipping wide. Even as it connected, the tall Clocker was on me. I caught the first blow against my left shoulder and my entire arm went numb. I rolled, got to my feet, and lashed out with one foot. It caught the Knuckle-knocker on the thigh and slowed him, allowing me time to catch my breath.

"Max Wilson," I said hoarsely. "Didn't he tell you about me?"

The big man lashed out again, and I avoided the blow, though with difficulty. Something caused me to turn then, and I saw the small Clocker behind me, swinging a tree branch. It connected, and I felt myself falling. The small Clocker, I noticed, had never stopped grinning—or speaking gibberish.

I woke up just outside the Jesuit mission they'd converted into their headquarters. I hurt—I'd been worked over by the Knuckle-knocker until I was a mass of livid bruises. I groaned when somebody splashed a bucket of water over me.

"You must be Hillman," I heard somebody say. I rolled over and peered through a swollen eye. The speaker was thirtyish, a walking corpse. The death-clock on his forehead stood out starkly, a teardrop of alabaster.

Standing up was painful, but I managed it.

"You Wilson?"

"Yeah."

"Fine welcome you arranged."

Wilson ignored the sarcasm. "You said in your letter you wanted to be a Clocker. That right?"

I nodded.

"Why?"

"I wrote you why. I deserted from the Army about a month ago. I'm tired of hiding, tired of running. I don't figure I owe the Triumvirate anything. Besides," I managed a crooked grin, "being a Clocker seemed like the ultimate trip."

Wilson stepped up close. He had the blackest eyes I had ever seen.

"Let me tell you what you're getting into, Hillman. You see this death-clock?" He touched the teardrop on his brow. "It's set to go off just over a year from now. It was originally set for ten years. It can't be removed and it can't be delayed. It's tamper-proof."

I nodded my understanding. "It has a timing device

and two milligrams of pi-dalinol—a real rocket. Death in less than a minute."

He grinned at me. "You ever had pi-dalinol, Hillman?"

I returned the grin, staring directly into the other's eyes. "Can't get it anywhere on the mainland. I know. I've tried."

"That's right." Wilson chuckled, then glanced around. I looked around when Wilson did, and several of the Clockers began to laugh. Wilson turned back to me.

"You sure you want to be a Clocker?"

"That's what I came here for," I replied. I did not mention what else I had come there for.

Wilson raised black eyebrows and touched me lightly on the arm. "Okay, man. Welcome."

"Thanks." I looked around dubiously.

"You still don't get it, do you?" the Clocker boss said. "You're already a Clocker. Feel your forehead."

Now I understood the amusement among the Clockers. They'd put on the device while I was unconscious. I fingered the area over my right eye, felt the hard ridged presence of the clock.

Wilson slapped me on the back. "What Dillon and Craft gave you out there in the woods—that was your initiation."

I grunted and felt the various parts of my swollen anatomy. "I'm glad they weren't mad at me," I said finally.

Wilson rattled off further instructions. If I had a dispute with another Clocker I could settle it in the knuckle-knocker ring. There were a lot of crazy stories about Clocker women. Most of them weren't true. Poaching another man's woman was a cardinal sin.

Craft, the big Knuckle-knocker, was assigned to show me around. He guided me through the mission, got me a room, and brought up my duffle bag. He showed none of the stark animal fury he'd exhibited earlier.

"No hard feelings about the initiation?" he asked.

I shook my head. "Glad it's over, is all."

Craft's eyes dwelt on my face. "Almost over," he corrected slowly.

"Almost?"

"Right."

I felt more than a little uneasy. I glanced quickly around the spare, white-washed room. There was no escape. I tried to shake off the trapped feeling.

"Sit down," Craft told me. He pointed to a stool with one scarred hand. I sat down.

"We been here twelve years," the Clocker said. "Every once in a while somebody comes here from the outside, like you, and they think they know about Clockers."

I opened my mouth and then shut it again.

"Right," Craft said, looking at me. "All anyone knows, we got this clock in our head going to kill us. That's truth. It means we live for each day, man. We live each minute like it was our last. Somebody duels us and he could split off the top of our head."

He paused for a moment before continuing.

"You seen Dillon out there today on the trail, talking ramble—that comes from pi, man."

"Pi?"

"Pi-dalinol. It affects some Clockers like that. Dillon, he's a special case. He's been taking pi for years."

I ran my hands through my hair and tried to absorb what he was saying.

"I thought pi kills," I said. "Like in the clocks."

"Right. Dillon, he's been taking it cut with sugar. About a quarter mil."

I raised my eyebrows and Craft gave me a glacial smile. I immediately had a horrible suspicion.

"Right," Craft said. "That's for you, brother. You gonna have a piece of pi."

*   *   *

There were about forty Clockers on the island, half of them women and children. None of the children had clocks.

I wandered around the mission—slowly, to ease the aches and bruises. I was looking for one Clocker in particular. I found him fishing for flounder off a rock shelf. He was about thirty-five or so, with wide-set gray eyes and dark curly hair. Toby Roberson.

I was a little behind and above him. I sat down on a flat stone and watched him fish. The second part of the initiation worried me more than the first had. Craft said they'd come for me at dusk. I hoped I wouldn't give anything away while under the drug.

Toby glanced around, saw me, waved a hand. I waved back. He didn't look like someone who'd lost his senses. He looked happy, fulfilled.

There was sudden movement to my right. A woman came into view and strolled toward the water's edge. Her face was heart-shaped, with high cheekbones. Her hair was dark, with a hint of auburn. The death-clock on her brow contrasted sharply with her deep tan.

She and Toby engaged in friendly conversation. I couldn't make out what was said, but I heard laughter. They were enjoying themselves. Neither acted as though Clocker life was a hardship.

I stood and picked my way through the maze of sharp-edged stones. At my approach both Toby and the woman fell silent.

"Hello," I said. I was interested to see if Toby would see through my disguise. He didn't; he gave a relaxed nod.

The girl returned my greeting, then looked at me, her eyes lingering on the bruises. When it came, her smile was genuine, fully given.

"You're the new one—I heard about you. I'm Mindy. Welcome to Clock Island."

"If I live through the welcome—thanks." I gave her my name and a rueful smile.

"If you were worried about living a long life, you wouldn't be a Clocker," the girl reminded me. She grinned. "You look tough. You'll make it."

I looked out over the water. "You two seem happy enough. Ever have second thoughts about being Clockers?"

Toby shook his head, glanced at the girl, smiled.

"No."

I gave them both a look that was frankly disbelieving.

"There are a lot of things about it people from the outside don't understand," the girl said. Her mouth curved defensively. "A feeling of unity, for instance."

"Maybe," I said doubtfully. "Unified as far as the dueling ring."

"Unified in purpose, even there. That's our court." She shrugged. "At least we don't have the hypocrisy found everywhere else in the world."

"How about the children? You want this life for them, too?"

Her manner got a trifle cooler. "Why not? We're all born with a death sentence hanging over us. The Clockers have just put a tangible date to it. You'll find out each day is sweeter, more precious, because of your clock."

I quoted, " 'I am a time binder . . . with seconds of diamonds, minutes of gold.' "

"That's God's own truth!"

I said nothing. The girl was obviously sincere, and I doubted I could change her mind. There were several corollaries to the Clocker culture, of course. I thought briefly of the motorcycle fraternities and their self-destructive way of life, complete with brawls, ritual murders, and clashes with police. Were the Clockers really so different? In their defense, they did not thrust their lifestyle on others, they avoided the debilitating agues of extreme age, and their lives, while short, were certainly not boring.

I drew no conclusions. It seemed as sane as living under the thumb of the Triumvirate. I nodded to Mindy and Toby and followed the beach around as far as the lagoon. There I shucked off my clothes and slid into the water. It felt good against my skin, against the purple weals Craft had put there; it eased the hurt. I swam until the sun disappeared beyond the promontory. At dusk, Craft had said, the second part of my initiation would begin.

The mission courtyard was filled with Clockers. I saw Craft and Mindy watching, and threw them a lopsided grin. In another knot of Clockers someone began to speak in tongues. I recognized the voice; it was the Mumble-mocker, Dillon.

Max Wilson strode toward me. In one skeletal hand he held a mug half full of what looked like fruit juice. I guessed the initiation was about to begin.

He studied me for several seconds, and the throng grew quiet. Then, as if in a ritual, he passed me the mug. "Drink it all, Hillman, if you would truly be a Clocker."

I drained it in one gulp, handed the mug back to him.

"How long before I feel it?"

Wilson shrugged. "Half hour, mebbe less. The effect will last until daybreak."

I felt a hand on my shoulder and looked up into the Knuckle-knocker's eyes.

"There was half a mil of pi in that mug," Craft told me. "Pretty soon now you'll begin to feel it. Just let it take you, man. Don't fight it." There was genuine concern in the big man's eyes.

"Thanks."

"Listen," Craft said quickly. "This island, it's yours til

dawn. Nobody is going to challenge what you do tonight. You're not responsible, got it?"

I looked at him. "Not responsible. 'Kay."

Fifteen minutes later I felt ill. My stomach began to cramp and I doubled over in anguish. When the pain passed, there were no Clockers in the courtyard. The big oak doors leading into the mission had been locked, bolted. I could feel the impact of forty pairs of eyes, staring out at me.

Instead of getting darker, the night got lighter. I could see details clearly. I stood up. I felt strong, unburdened of needs of the flesh. I felt as a god must feel.

I left the courtyard and ran along the trail leading down to the beach. Small animals were caught in webs of light fibres, their movements slowed and fed into my brain. I laughed at their clumsy movements. I looked up. Above me stars began to blink on and off and change colors.

I spent an eternity at the ocean's edge, watching the waters dance and churn. Everywhere I looked, there was life. It was rampant on the rusty sand, soup-like in the saline sea.

The need for motion overtook me. I ran to the top of the promontory. The wind whipped my hair. My body did not tire, but instead grew stronger. I feared nothing—I could not be harmed. The sky above me became too bright. I could see beyond it to the depths of space.

God spoke, in no language I knew. I cried out, in no language I remembered.

Mumble-mocking, I looked down. The fibres of light caught human movement, magnified it. Dillon looked up, smiling, his eyes riveted on me, though the island was sprawled in shadow.

I sniffed the wind. I smelled blood and death and salt. Dillon stood in shadow, silent, waiting.

We met in the hour before dawn, our powers at their peak. We grappled, and Dillon threw me into the ocean. The warm sea strengthened me. I rose out of it and struck Dillon across the face. Knuckle-knocking, I broke the other's nose, unleashing a sudden river of blood.

Dillon rolled, came up behind me, and snaked his arms about my chest. He began to squeeze.

The brightness of the night began to fade. The sky closed in, sounds of the earth began to pound uncomprehendingly in my ears. I heard Dillon mumble-mocking, and felt the constrictor grip grow tighter.

We stood on a rise, where below the sea beat a sullen tattoo against a spine of rocks. I staggered forward, dragging Dillon with me. Deliberately, I twisted my body, throwing myself into space, taking the other with me. When we struck, Dillon's grip loosened. Stars whirled erratically in their orbits, fog brushed my mind with blackness. The universe vanished.

I woke up. Frothy water lapped against one arm. My face was against a flat, uneven surface. I raised my head high enough to look and saw it was a broken piece of stone. I blinked. The sun was a high sphere, the sky a vivid blue.

"You just about bought it, man," I heard someone say. I looked up again, saw Craft's scarred hands and angular features.

"Dillon. . . !"

"Yeah, we know," Craft said moodily. "He had his chance. Last night he took three quarters of a mil. By rights he should have killed you, man. Instead, you killed him. That's okay; he only had a couple of months left anyway. Why he tried it, probably." The big Clocker dipped up water and splashed it on my face.

There were no broken bones. I was able to walk back to the mission. I felt battered, bone tired. I got down a little soup and then staggered wearily up the steps to my room. I threw myself across the bed and was asleep within seconds.

When I woke up for the second time, it was late in the afternoon. I splashed water on my face and went downstairs. I felt dizzy, depressed. There was a hurt within that ate at me.

Craft was waiting. He took one look at my face and dug out a bottle of whiskey. He poured me a liberal shot.

"This will make things a little brighter, man."

I took a gulp of the whiskey, felt it begin to spread through my middle.

"Thanks. Is the initiation over?"

The big Clocker nodded shortly. "It's over. Glad to have you with us."

I finished the whiskey and walked outside. The island was still hushed in the afterglow of the day. The sun was gone, sunk below the horizon, leaving only a few golden clouds to mark its passage. I sat down on a fallen log, stared out to sea.

I heard movement, then a voice. "If you want to be alone, just say the word."

I looked up. Max Wilson was watching me gravely, his cadaver-thin body propped against the boll of a tree.

"No," I said. "It's fine."

We talked a while, and he proved to be an able philosopher, but his casuistry was not wholly convincing. Probably, I told myself, because it devolved into a matter of taste.

Then he left me, and still I sat, letting the dimness envelop me. And I thought, suddenly, of a time twelve years before.

"*You have a visitor, Gilliam.*" Mrs. McClosky's rasping tones were the loudest sound in the library wing.

"*Who?*"

"*His name is Dean Markham. He's a very famous man.*"

I was aware of another presence, with an erect, almost military bearing. Blond, close-cut hair, piercing hazel eyes.

"You'll leave us," the man said, and Mrs. McClosky closed the door though she never took orders from anyone.

"How old are you, Gil?"

"Fourteen."

"Your guardian says you're always in trouble."

"Mrs. McClosky?" I snorted, then looked at him more closely. "Who're you?"

He paused for three or four seconds, drew a step nearer, said quietly, "I'm your father."

I stared. "Yeah, sure."

"I mean it. I've spent a lot of time and money tracking you down. I never even knew your mother was pregnant; she never told me. But there were records, and medical tests that are 99 percent certain." He smiled faintly. "I almost found you at Corsorian's farm, but you ran away before I got there." His face looked strange. "Not that I blame you."

Something twisted inside me. My chest hurt from not breathing. I said, "I don't believe you."

"Maybe not," he replied. "But you will. You have a brother, too. His name is Chester. I think you'll like each other."

"The hell you say!"

He gave a quiet grin, and then a nod. "The hell I say."

Full dark found me in the sheltered harbor, looking over the few boats the Clockers kept tied up there. Afterward I wandered slowly along the beach, my mind in turmoil, reliving the previous night. I was so absorbed I almost bumped into the girl.

"Sorry," I said. "I guess I wasn't watching where I was going."

"No harm done," Mindy said. I caught a glimpse of white teeth in the darkness.

We walked for a while in silence, feeling the wind off the sea. At last I stopped and looked at her.

"Have you been all through that, too?"

"You mean pi?"

"Yes."

"Of course. All Clockers go through it."

"And did you feel . . . like I feel now?"

She touched me lightly on the arm. "Why do you think I came down to the beach? Nobody is left alone the first night after initiation."

Above us the stars glittered coldly. So cold and so cruel they sent shivers up my spine. I slumped down on the sand, and after a moment the girl sat down beside me.

"What I felt last night," I said, "I want that back." There was a vast regret within me.

"Yes," Mindy replied slowly, "I know. And that's what you'll have—when your clock runs down."

I didn't say anything. Almost, I thought, it would be worth it. To be truly a god. I no longer wondered why Clockers were content to count their days.

I looked sideways at the dim shape of the girl. "Dillon had been taking pi regularly. Why was it he had a private supply?"

She shrugged. "Back on the mainland he was a research chemist. He discovered pi-dalinol. We made an exception in his case."

We sat for a while longer, watching the slate and obsidian shadows of the sea creep inward with the tide. I felt her hand on my arm, then, and I turned and reached for her. Almost, but not quite, it made me forget the night before.

"*Hillman,*" was a voice crying . . . and "*Hillman,*" was the sound of pulsing surf. And "*Hillman,*" was the sweet, sated, heavy breath of woman.

I woke up, remembering. It was seven o'clock in the morning. In two hours the skimmer would pass the island on its return run. I emptied the contents of my duffle bag onto the bed and pocketed what looked like an ordinary pen. I put three more in my shirt pocket and folded the duffle bag flat, finally stowing it under my shirt.

The other Clockers paid no attention when I walked through the mission and down the path toward the beach. There was no reason why they should.

I waited by the shelf of rock until Toby showed up, his fishing pole slung over one shoulder.

"Morning, Toby."

"Morning," he said cheerfully. He plunked himself down beside me and baited his hook. Almost casually I reached out and touched him with one of the pens. A needle darted out, ruptured the skin. A quantity of drug was flushed into his bloodstream.

His eyes rounded and he tried to get up. Within moments his knees gave way and he collapsed in a heap. I caught him before he could slide off the shelf.

"Toby . . . speak to me!"

He looked at me. He blinked his eyes.

"What . . ?"

I held up the pen. "Nothing to worry about. It's a standard truth-getter. You'll be all right in a half-hour."

He leaned wearily against one of the flat stones. His eyes flicked over me, accepted the inevitable.

"Who are you? What do you want?"

I gave him a quick grin. "You know me, Toby. I'm Gil Warren. I want to know what you can tell me about the Triumvirate. Who they are—what they're like."

He looked at me closely, the drug taking hold and slackening the muscles in his face. At length he shook his head and shrugged his shoulders.

"I've been conditioned," he said in a flat monotone.

"Sandone did it before he went Up-Top. I can't tell you anything about the PPS Project."

Give Sandone a point—he was thorough. I hadn't wanted to use anything stronger on Toby, but there wasn't time to be squeamish. I touched him with another of the pens and watched his face tighten into little knots of muscle that worked against each other. It was painful, and painful to watch, but the second drug was guaranteed to break down even the most stubborn will. What I didn't like to think about was the aftermath. Toby would have nightmares for years.

It took an hour. Sandone had set his screens deep. By the time I had broken through, Toby's eyes were dead, all signs of intelligence obliterated. I looked at him, and shivered, and thought of what the Gods would do to me if they ever ran me to ground. Toby, I thought, had no complaints.

"Who are they?" I asked him. "What are their names?" I wiped saliva from his chin.

"Bra . . . Branham . . . Heywood . . . Morse . . ." Toby strained against an inner tension, the breath puffing out of him. The last of Sandone's barriers fell audibly, bursting from his lips in frothy bubbles.

"Tell me about Branham," I said.

It took twenty minutes to pick him dry. When I was through, I pulled him farther back from the shelf's edge and propped his limp form carefully between two stones. I had no war with Toby.

When I straightened up, I found myself face to face with Mindy. Confusion and anger had drawn her features into rigid lines. She turned half away, her mouth opening to scream—the last thing I wanted, the thing I could least afford.

I said, "Sorry, love," and struck her savagely with my right fist. I paused only for the time it took to ascertain that she was breathing normally, and then I was off at a sloping run, headed for the far end of the island. My leg ached dully, but I had no time to delay. I was thankful it was too early for most Clockers to be up and about. In another hour I would have been challenged for what I was doing—what I had done.

It did not take long to reach the ocean at the island's tip. I stopped long enough to regain my breath and dig the duffle bag out of my shirt. I unfolded it and reached inside. I drew out the lining, effectively doubling the length of the bag.

I stopped to listen, but the only sounds were the raucous screech of seagulls. I had time, still. I tugged another pen from my pocket and touched its end to a hidden valve on the side of the bag. There was a hiss of air and the duffle bag inflated into a unwieldly-looking one-man dory. I lifted it and had taken barely two steps when I caught the movement from the corner of my eyes. I dropped the dory and turned, my body already in a crouch.

Ten feet from me the big Knuckle-knocker stood watching, his face expressionless, eyes dead.

"I was down by the boats this morning," he said slowly. "Somebody put a hole in each of them. You, man. Why?"

I shrugged, and waited. The big Clocker's eyes roved silently over the small boat and out at the blue-green water. At first he appeared puzzled, then his expression hardened as he understood. I saw his fists curl into ridged hammers.

I set myself. The big man possessed prodigious strength and uncanny speed. If I had any advantage at all it was in experience and slightly faster reflexes.

He came in at a crouch, his face impassive, showing neither fear nor anger. His left fist shot out for a smashing punch to the midsection. I dropped back half a step, caught the out-thrust arm, and heaved. Off balance, he crashed heavily to the sand. He recovered quickly, however, and came in swinging.

I ducked a man-killing right and drove my stiffened fingers into the soft flesh just beneath his ribs. The big Clocker grunted and bent over. I raised a knee to meet his chin.

He wasn't through. One massive hand caught me by the wrist. I broke two of his fingers before I could escape. I aimed another kick at his chin, saw it connect. He fell backward, unconscious.

Breathing heavily, I pushed the boat into the water and vaulted in, taking care not to overbalance it. I glanced at my watch—I was none too early.

Paddling with both hands, I maneuvered the small boat into deep water half a mile or more from the island. Aready I could hear the banshee shriek of the approaching skimmer. As soon as I could make it out, I took the last pen out of my pocket and broke off one end. A blue and yellow flare arced high into the air, causing the skimmer to alter its course toward me.

Captain Marsh helped me aboard. Two crewman even took the time to rescue my boat. The captain as well as the crew stared openly at the death-clock on my brow.

"I've heard of those things," Captain Marsh said apprehensively. "If you tamper with it, you're a dead man."

I gave him a faint grin. "It's not set to go off for ten years," I assured him. As the engines revved, I slumped wearily onto a deck chair. Staring out over the water, I massaged my leg and thought about the Gods Up-Top.

No longer were they faceless, energies without form. They had names, pasts, weaknesses. Perhaps they could be beaten. I leaned my head against the padding. A single thought pushed its way into my consciousness and I grinned darkly.

An old admonition.

Know thy enemy . . .

Chapter Eleven

There were three men sitting in an abandoned office of the Consolidated Electric Company in Richmond, Virginia, the windows overlooking the James River shuttered, nailed shut.

One of the men held a gun, an ugly-looking long-barreled automatic. The sound suppressor threaded onto the end of the barrel would reduce the sound of the shot by more than two-thirds.

"We're going to ask you some questions," another of the men said. "We want straight answers. If we think you're hedging, holding back, we'll just leave and let Clint take care of you."

The man doing the talking was fortyish, taller than the others, with a wiry build and a full head of gray hair. He was *not* the one in charge, though. That one was a black man, sitting with his legs propped on a desk, his eyes thoughtful, his attention unwavering.

"Do you understand what I've just said?"

"You said if I don't answer truthfully you'll sic Clint on me," I answered, studying the black man surreptitiously. He was the man I had to convince, not the gray-haired one; and certainly not Clint, who looked like he had not yet advanced to Speak-and-Spell.

The three were members of an anti-Triumvirate underground, and as such, I needed their help. Though exactly what could be accomplished was, at the moment, conjecture.

I had heard of them through Sam Portner. One of the hobos who came through his camp had let a name slip. After Sam found out who I was, he suggested I investigate. There was, he said, power in numbers. And so now, at long last, I was investigating.

And I'd succeeded, if looking down the barrel of a gun could be deemed success.

The light inside the room was from a battery-powered reading lamp from army surplus, an irony I appreciated even if the three did not. The Consolidated Electric Company had long since been bankrupt, their turbines silenced; not so much as a joule passed through this building's power lines.

"What's your name?"

"Brent Hawkins," I said. That name matched the driver's license I'd stolen, as did the photograph I had put on it. The photograph—and I—bore a scar over the right eye, a legacy of the Deathclockers. The clock itself was now above Everest, in the spaces reached through Sandone's lens.

"How did you hear of Project High Eagle?"

"Is what what you call it? It sounds more than vaguely military."

"Just answer the question."

I said, "There was a man I met on a train—an empty freight car, if you must know—who said there was something finally being done . . ."

"His name—!" The interrogator prodded me with a piece of curtain rod he'd found on the floor. I knocked it aside and stared at him. "Is this the way you treat all recruits?"

The gray-haired man looked at the black man, then put aside the curtain rod. "Who was the man?" he asked in quieter tones.

I was sitting on the edge of a footstool, and was therefore lower than my inquisitors. It made good sense psychologically, and I didn't resent it. But my back was getting tired, and the chairs they were sitting in looked very comfortable.

I said, "He called himself Petey Joe. No last name. He liked his liquor and he carried a lot of little glassine bags."

"Goddamn it, I told you we should have taken care of Pete!" The gray-haired man rounded on his superior, anger suffusing his features.

"If it's any consolation," I said, talking to the black man, "Petey Joe isn't around any more. He fell under a train as he was trying to board it."

"We used Pete as a courier once," the black man said, speaking for the first time. "Perhaps Doug is right, maybe we should have 'taken care' of him." His voice was cultured, educated, cold.

"He was a harmless little guy," I told him. "He just got high once in a while."

"High enough to give us away," Doug pointed out vehemently.

The questions went on, and my position on the stool got more uncomfortable. I answered readily enough, though, and Clint, sensing perhaps that his talents would not be needed, put his gun away.

"What kind of work do you do, Brent?"

"I was a soldier," I said.

"What branch?"

"Infantry and artillery." I had researched the real Brent Hawkins enough to know his service record. It tallied closely enough with my own. I said nothing about the dozen or so other occupational niches I'd fitted myself into.

"Neither of those will do much good against the Triumvirate," the black man said. He took his feet off the desk and sat up a little straighter. "We need engineers, physicists, chemists."

"What for?"

He shook his head. "That's later, if your story checks out. Right now, we're interested in how *you* can help us."

I could help them a lot, of course. Like give them the names and habits of the Triumvirate. But I kept my mouth shut. I wasn't yet convinced that undergrounds were the answer. Mark had said the Gods were watching some of the underground groups. For all I knew, Project High Eagle was on their list.

On the other hand, if I didn't give them *something*, they'd feel obliged to have Clint unlimber his gun again.

So I said, "I spent time working with some dockrats on Fanny Six. Nice bunch of guys. They let me crawl around inside one of the Observation Vehicles. I *might* be able to break in on the command chain."

"Oh?" The black man gave me a look of reappraisal. Fanny VI was a potent force. If it could somehow be taken over—or disabled—it would be a coup for the underground. The Gods had never used the mechanized army and, at last report, it was still in Africa. Still, the *threat* of it—

The three of them moved away and whispered to one another for a time. Clint stole occasional glances at me, his eyes beetled disapprovingly. When they were finished, they resumed their former positions.

"We're going to keep you isolated for a few days," the gray-haired man said. "From time to time we'll ask you questions—about your past, about the units under Fanny Six. If your answers are satisfactory, we'll have other uses for you."

"And then. . . ?"

The black man raised a hand to stop the other from replying. "We're only a cell," he said. "The smallest unit of an underground organization. That means we can't betray our colleagues—even if we're caught—because we know only one member of *another* cell. Do you follow that?"

"It makes sense," I said.

"Good. Then you'll appreciate the fact that decisions aren't made at this level. We'll bump the information about you up-line, of course. In the meantime, you go with Clint, do as he says."

Clint took me down four floors and deposited me in a sandstone cellar that looked as though it flooded whenever it rained. There was a couch along one wall, a hot-plate, a pair of cheap chairs. The cabinet over the sink contained coffee, canned beans, and a smelly wedge of yellow cheese. A portable television occupied a niche on the wall.

I said, "What's the difference between this and the Bastille?"

"What's a Bastille?" Clint asked. He stood in the doorway, hands loose at his sides. Even without his gun, he would have made a formidable opponent.

"Never mind. Are you staying with me?"

"No." Clint produced a large key and proceeded to lock the door, peering in at me through one of the tiny windows.

"Wait a minute!" I called. "How long am I going to be stuck in here?"

His heels made clicking sounds as he walked away, and I found myself shuddering. Except for the television and food, I thought, I could as well have been back in Jake Corsorian's root cellar.

I tried the door. It was oak, thick and heavy, with ironwork all over it.

With a shrug, I stretched out on the couch, closed my eyes, tried to fall asleep.

My sleep, when it came, was uneasy. I dreamed of something that had happened years before, when Mark and I were boys. In a fit of anger he had pitched me into a river. Then, seeing me struggle, he'd jumped in and pulled me to shore, using his long arms and legs as though born to the water.

He said afterwards: "Nothing bad will ever happen to you while I'm around." And then, arms around each other, we'd walked home.

I woke up sweating.

A day later Clint and Doug came to see me, asking for diagrams of the Obs-Vehicle. I drew them while Clint restocked my larder. When they were ready to go away, I said, "I really don't *like* this place. Isn't here somewhere else I can stay?"

"This is safe," Doug said, and turned away.

"Wait, dammit!"

They turned, gave me a look.

"The black man," I said, "what is his name?"

"Morrison," Clint said, before Doug could stop him.

I took advantage of it. "Yeah, Morrison. I want to talk to him."

"I'll tell him," Doug said. He gave me a smile that meant maybe yes, maybe no.

The second night I lay staring at the ceiling, watching a spider make his way across an expanse of peeling plaster. In my mind I was seeing something else—Alicia Fannon's face, terrified, at the top of the gallery. Then my brother's hurtling body. It ran like a loop of film in my head, running over, again and again. Where was Alicia Fannon now? No one had seen her since that night. Had she been captured, taken Up-Top? Or was she like me, a fugitive?

I left that after some minutes and thought about Morrison and his minions and the cell of which I was a part. Literally and figuratively. There was something I was missing . . . something . . .

It took about an hour, and at first it didn't make sense. And then it did.

"Your sketches check out," Morrison said. He seated himself on one of the chairs, looked across at me.

"I expected them to," I replied.

Clint, arms folded across his massive chest, was standing by the door. The gray-haired man was not in evidence.

Morrison indicated the room with a wave of his hand. "Sorry about this, but we do have to take precautions."

Wryly, I asked, "Have *you* ever stayed here?"

"No." His face was expressionless.

"Don't. You won't like it."

He turned, regarded me, looked away again. "Doug said you wanted to see me. What about?"

I was seated on the couch, my legs pulled up in a yogic posture. I'd been practicing it off and on for the past day or so. Now, watching the black man's face, I said, "The underground—it's set up by the government, isn't it?"

His eyes narrowed just enough for me to be sure. He was good, though; it didn't go any further than that.

"What do you mean?"

I said, "Overtly, the government is under the thumb of the Triumvirate—though the PR men are calling it 'cooperation.' *Covertly*, however, there are resistance groups being set up—all over the country, maybe, and funded by the military. Like this one." I paused a moment to watch his reaction. "Powerful as they are, the Gods can't watch everybody."

"That's an interesting theory," the black man said. He stood, moved about the room, lit a cigarette. He looked at me.

"Like one?"

"Thanks." I took it, let him light it, then blew a perfect smoke ring. "*You* gave it away," I said.

He looked interested, so I went on. "If you were of the Caucasian persuasion, you would probably have had a white area on your left index finger—from an academy ring. What are you, anyway? A captain? A major?"

"You're boring me, Hawkins."

"I don't think so." I paused long enough to blow another smoke ring. "And there is that cockamamie name: Project High Eagle. That *had* to come off a computer data base programmed by the Army."

"Anything else?"

"Sorry to annoy you, but there *were* one or two things. Clint's weapon is more or less standard issue—although that sound suppressor is not. And at first I thought that lamp upstairs was army surplus. It isn't, though, is it?"

Morrison smoked his cigarette and quietly observed the spider web that had been three days in the spinning.

"You spend your time down here figuring all that out?" he remarked at last.

"There wasn't a whole lot else to do."

"I suppose not."

He shook two or three more cigarettes out of his pack and placed them on top of the television set. "We'll have word on you by morning," he said. "Until then, take it easy."

"Sure. You, too."

When they were gone I got up from the couch and made myself some coffee on the hotplate. Presently, cup in hand, I contemplated another aspect of the underground.

Morrison had said they were looking for engineers, physicists, and chemists. The purpose? Somewhere, it came to me, the resistance might have in mind a missile—one that could carry a suitable warhead and achieve a high orbit.

They were planning to blow Up-Top—and the Gods—right out of the heavens.

I poured myself a second cup of coffee, had a sudden disquieting thought. If they *were* Army, and I was now convinced they were, then they would have access to military records. Said records would reveal details about Brent Hawkins that I wasn't aware of.

—And that would be my death warrant.

Coffee cup in hand, I approached the door. I could, of course, use a micro-grenade on it—like the one I'd used to kill Fannon—and simply blow it off its hinges. But unless I was mistaken, that would bring Clint with his large gun. There were other ways, quieter ways, to exit the room.

I examined the edge of the jamb where the door's lock fit. It was not quite flush, and a glint of steel revealed where the deadbolt was. A small quantity of a certain acid would eat through it in an hour or so; fortunately, obtaining the acid was not a problem.

While it worked, I finished the coffee, and one of the three cigarettes Morrison had left. Then, resuming my yoga-like posture, I watched what passed for television.

It took an hour and a half instead of an hour. But the door opened when I put my shoulder to it, snapping what remained of the deadbolt, swinging creakily back on its hinges.

I climbed two flights of stairs, found a broken window through which I could smell fresh breezes. Carefully, I removed the two or three obstructing boards.

Easing my way out of the window, I wished Project High Eagle good luck. They'd probably shut this "safe house" down, now that I had compromised it. But they had ample funding, and they'd find others. And what the hell—maybe they'd succeed.

In the meantime, I'd do what *I* could. Alone.

Fifteen minutes later I crossed the James River; the Consolidated Electric Company was simply another deep shadow on the far shore.

Chapter Twelve

Bar Harbor in the winter.

The humidity there hugs like three days of slept-in clothes, raw and unforgiving. The cold penetrates to bone. You spend your waking hours ten inches from a roaring pot-bellied stove and your sleeping time between layers of goosedown quilt. You drink scalding coffee for breakfast, lunch, and dinner—and you pray to Persephone for an early spring.

Skeeter John Branham, in turned-back sleeves and open-throated shirt, looked at me and laughed. He was a small, squat phenomenon; an engine with an out-of-phase thermostat, muscles that appeared to be steel cables, and glinting cheerful eyes of a peculiar washed-out blue.

He was, from all I'd been able to guess, a crook—although no one had ever caught him crooking.

He sat now behind his dingy gray-steel desk and looked up at me. Outside the wind howled and grains of mixed sleet and ice rattled against the window glass.

"You get number three cleaned up yet?"

"Yes," I answered dutifully. Skeeter John maintained a dozen cottages that perched on the cliffs and faced out to sea. I worked for him, cleaning them, cutting fresh firewood, doing odd repairs. They had to be a front, those cottages; he couldn't have made a living from them.

None of it made sense. He lived in one of the cottages and let the big house on the point sit empty. He'd built an office off the side of the cottage away from the sea and behind that he'd put in a separate generating station. What for, I didn't know. It had not been used in the short time I'd worked there.

He scratched his head and gave me a grin.

"You going to town?"

"If it's okay with you."

He nodded. "Nobody will be coming here in this weather. I'll drop you if you want to wait."

"Thanks," I said. For the past two Friday evenings I had spent an hour or two at a local bar. Where Skeeter John went after he dropped me off was a mystery, but he always carried a heavy-seeming briefcase with him, returning with it hanging limp and empty at the end of his arm.

In my own small cottage, with the curtains drawn and the fire built up, I went through the ritual that so far had kept me out of the hands of the Triumvirate.

My hair was blond now, and thinned across the crown. My nose resembled a pliant potato and leaned to the left. There was a small scar on my forehead where a death-clock had once rested. I looked at the reflection in the mirror, saw nothing that reminded me of Gilliam Warren. I saw instead a broken derelict face, a composite of all the hopeless indigent men I'd met in a lifetime. I touched up my eyebrows with toner and gave myself a crooked grin. I was Scott Chesbro, a name I'd picked off a tombstone outside Lawrence, Kansas.

Knuckles thundered on the door just as I was finishing.

"Come on, Scotty! Move your butt!"

I put the toner in the kit with my spare faces, rolled

it up, and hid it in the hollow bedpost—a bedpost that had not *been* hollow when I'd started working there. Then I shrugged into my heavy seaman's jacket, wrapped a scarf around my neck, and went out into the night.

He had the briefcase tucked in beside him, as always. I gave it a glance, climbed in, and fastened my seatbelt. Before I was finished, Skeeter John had the little electric spinning around in front of the row of cottages and down the hill toward town. The swing of the lights gave a glimpse of ice-glazed trees, a stark wintry vista that hung on, though April was fast approaching.

"Business pick up in the spring?" I asked. We'd had one renter in the last three weeks, an artist who had wanted to paint some gloomy beach scenes. I'd seen his finished canvases, and he had been good. But he hadn't managed to capture the utter desolation of the Maine coast.

Skeeter John shrugged, and barreled the little car around a curve. He drove too fast, but he handled the vehicle as though he'd been born behind a wheel.

"Why? You thinking of staying on?"

"Maybe."

He raised his eyebrows and said, "Hmmm," and looked out at the sleet and rain. It continued to fall, faster than ever.

"People are scared," he said after a moment. "They'll probably stick close to home, instead of traveling."

"Because of what's going on Up-Top?"

"Yeah."

"What do you think will happen?"

He gave me a quick glance. "That's hard to say. It sure looks like they're calling the shots—whoever the hell *they* are." His mouth tightened and his face looked grim—that same grimness I'd seen reflected in faces from California to Maine. It was a kind of sick despair, the kind of look men get when their future is no longer their own to command.

He dropped me off at the corner of Belvidere and Maple, where, catercornered across the street, was a huge empty warehouse and in its lee, like a solvent younger brother, Danelon's Bar.

He gave me a grin. "See you in the morning. Don't stack them too high."

"No." I returned the grin and watched the car rocket off through the storm. Too fast, I thought, but he did a thing then, his foot going from accelerator to brake to accelerator, and skated around the corner with the precision of a ballet movement.

I liked Danelon's, as much for its lack of pretensions as for anything else. Oh, it had its hundred-year-old fireplace and jackplaned tables, but Danelon didn't dwell on it overmuch. On Friday nights he imported college kids to sing ballads, and they sang for beer and tips, and sometimes for the fun of it.

When it was vacant, I used a booth at the rear of the bar. A door just behind it opened on a storage room full of empties. There was an exit there that opened on an alley.

The booth was unoccupied and I sat there sipping a beer, assessing the Friday-night crowd. It was lean for a weekend, running mostly to regulars. The weather probably had a lot to do with that.

"Howza boy, Scotty?" Danelon sat down across from me and made a bridge of his elbows, resting his chin in the interlocking trestle of his fingers.

"I'm doing fine," I answered. "But you got lousy weather here in the Harbor, Frank. It makes my bones ache." No lie, that. My left leg felt as though slow knives were working on it.

"How about a game?"

"Sure."

He went behind the bar and came back with a chess set made from thirty-caliber cartridge shells and we sorted out the men. Standard practice, I took white and one of his black knights. He'd beat me anyhow, but at least he was no longer giving me his queen.

"You staying on up at Skeeter John's?"

I shrugged. "We talked about it some. I guess it depends on business."

He laughed. "Not really. Skeeter never cares how many customers he has."

"I'm finding that out. Those cottages are the coldest, dreariest, *goddamnedest* places on the whole east coast. How does he manage to stay in business?"

"You're not the first to wonder that," Danelon said. Then he was quiet for a time. We moved our chess pieces and he captured one of my knights, making us even again. I accepted it as inevitable, sipped my beer, advanced a pawn.

Frank Danelon had lived in Bar Harbor for forty years, and in that time he'd seen many come and go. Skeeter John was different. He'd just laughed his cheerful laugh while he got rich, though no one knew just how he did that. He'd borrowed money, some of it from Danelon, to buy the point cottages. After two years he'd managed to pay it back—with a bonus. After that he always had money. Word got around that he was heavily into computer stocks with a side portfolio in Mexican oil.

Whatever it was he was doing, he was doing it right.

I asked about the big house, and Danelon said it was used just once a year.

"What's the occasion?"

"Family reunion. Five or six couples, lots of little kids running around. You know the kind."

"Skeeter John the only Branham left in the area?"

"There used to be a lot of them," Danelon said, looking at the board. "They lived on the flats south of town, did some fishing, some lobstering. All of them moved away but Skeeter John."

I conceded the game after an hour or so and we had

two more beers and listened to saloon sounds. Across the room a dark-haired girl sang of John Henry, that steel-driving man, and to our left three or four regulars were metering coins into a bowling machine. It was time for me to be getting back.

I got into my coat and tucked my scarf under my chin.

"See you, Frank," I said, and went through the front door into the tail-end of the sleet storm. Tucking my hands into my pockets, I was glad I had the wind at my back and no more than a couple of miles to walk.

I found him about a hundred yards from the line of cottages; somehow he'd made it that far. He was slumped across the steering yoke of the electric, his head resting at an angle on the window glass.

I made sure he was still alive, then moved him onto the passenger seat and drove the car the rest of the way to the point. I talked to him, but he didn't answer, his usually laughing eyes showing no spark of consciousness.

He was surprisingly hard and heavy, but I got him inside and into bed and took care of some of the more severe surface abrasions. Nothing seemed broken, but he was a livid bruise from his head to his waist. Somebody had done a professional job on him.

"Skeeter John?"

He paid no attention to me, and I observed that sometimes oblivion can be a blessing. I left him and went into the tiny, ill-equipped kitchen and made some chicken soup.

Sometime later I remembered the briefcase. I went out to the car and searched for it to no avail. Apparently whoever had beaten him had also taken the case.

I could have taken him to a doctor and made certain there were no internal injuries, but I didn't think he wanted that. Besides, it was attention-getting, and I needed anonymity. I found aspirin and painkillers in his medicine chest and got him to swallow them, along with a little of the soup. He didn't say anything in those few moments, but his eyes flickered over me in acknowledgement. Afterward he slept, and I poured myself half a glass of his best Scotch and sat in one of his chairs watching the sleet beat tympani against the window panes.

It was melancholy making.

I thought about Catherine and felt a hollow longing. I wanted to see her, if only for a moment. Catherine of the twinkling gray eyes. Catherine of the ineffable ageless smile. Almost, I picked up the phone and called her. Then I stopped and cursed myself for a fool and laughed grimly. The Gods would like me to do that. They would like that very much.

I still made the news occasionally, and every now and then they ran pictures of me on television. It was evident the Triumvirate had not given up their search. Would not. I grimaced and finished what remained of Skeeter John's Scotch. Fair's fair—I damned well hadn't given up mine.

I stood in front of him and said, "Welcome back."

His eyes were all right, but his lips had been split and they started bleeding again when he cracked a grin.

He said simply, "Thanks."

"*Por nada.* Get you something?"

"Water."

I watched him drink, and when he was through, I put the glass on the table beside him.

He said, "They were waiting for me about ten miles out of the Harbor. Four of them."

"That figures. You could have handled three."

He gave me a look. "You still want to stay on?"

"As what, a punching bag?"

The grin again. "I'll be ready for them next time. But I need you to ride shotgun. You've been in fights before, haven't you?"

"One or two."

I sat down in a chair and we stared at each other mask to mask, so to speak. One contused, one contrived.

"If it's not being too nosy," I said, "what is it I'd be shotgunning? By the way, I looked—your briefcase is missing."

"Help me up," he said. "I'll show you." And when he was on his feet, sweating, he said, "You come in with me and ten percent is yours."

"Ten percent of what?"

"Ten percent of all the money you'll ever need."

Then he showed me a switch hidden in one of the clothes closets. When I hit it the right way the whole closet suddenly began to descend. Skeeter John gave me a lopsided smile and gripped the crossbar.

When we stopped moving we were thirty feet underground in a smallish chamber lighted by forty-watt bulbs. Skeeter John touched some studs in a funny pattern and stepped out of the closet.

"That's a fail-safe," he said, pointing to the studs. "If you don't hit them just the right way the whole chamber will collapse on top of you. Remember that and be careful."

"I'll remember," I said, following at his heels.

The only thing noteworthy about the chamber was a three feet by six feet steel canister almost exactly in its middle. It was lined with rubber and one end of the thing was black and hollow.

"What is it?" I looked at it and then turned around and looked at Skeeter John. He was standing about six feet away with a gun in his hand. There was a shelf by his shoulder that held several more weapons.

"Sit down over there," he told me.

There was a table and chairs in one corner of the chamber. I went to it and sat.

He walked, slowly, around behind me. I could hear the rasping sound his breathing made as he considered the back of my head. I supposed if he shot it at this range, said head would burst apart like a melon.

"You have exactly two minutes to prove I can trust you," he said in even tones.

"What is this all about?"

"You're wasting time."

"What happens after two minutes?"

"I use this gun." I turned a little and he waggled the gun. Above it, his eyes weren't laughing at all.

I sat and thought until half a minute had ticked away and then I said: "I saved your life, remember? Another hour in your condition and you would have been cold meat."

"That's not enough." He grinned crookedly. "You've got no past, Scotty. You could be an inside man, for all I know. A con like that goes all the way back to the Pharaohs."

"Inside man for whom?"

He mulled it over for three seconds. "While they were working me over I heard one of them use the name Georgie. That would make it Fricci and his group."

"I don't know anybody named Georgie—or Fricci."

"That's what we're trying to determine," he replied grimly. "Right now what you've shown me isn't good enough. Who are you? Where do you come from?" He stopped, wiped sweat from his forehead with his free hand.

"I'm Scott Chesbro," I said. "I drift around a lot. I like to try different climates."

"Not good enough."

"Well, Christ! What *is* good enough?"

"You tell me." He was still suffering from the beating, still sweating. Induced paranoia? I had known a psychologist once who told me trauma and fatigue often duplicated aberrant thought patterns.

"Skeeter . . ."

"Twenty seconds," he said.

I waited five more seconds. "What if I saved your life again? Would that prove anything?"

"What do you mean?"

"Well, assume I have a method of killing you before you kill me. Let's say I don't use it—*ergo*, I save your life."

He laughed without mirth. "That's going to be a hard thing to prove. Because if you have something and don't use it you're going to end up dead."

"I suppose you're right," I said. But even as I spoke I was going into set, feeling the flow of Sandone's lens around me, the slopes of Everest above.

Chapter Thirteen

The technical name for it is *Polylux*. In powdered form it is intensely hypergolic, igniting instantly in any oxygen-rich atmosphere. The light emitted is on an order of several magnitudes greater than an equal weight of magnesium.

I sought for it among the varied things I'd pushed through the lens—pushed there against my need. I sought it, found it, pulled.

"Five seconds . . . four. . . ."

I was looking studiously at the floor when it materialized and exploded like a miniature blue sun. I was rolling over on the floor an instant later, listening to the *ping* of a bullet ricocheting off the chair I'd vacated.

After a moment I rose, eased out of my shoes, and went across the chamber to the shelf. I removed all the guns but one, pocketed that one, then crossed the chamber again so that I stood behind the metal canister.

"Drop the gun, Skeeter," I said, and put a shot to either side of him.

He fired immediately, reflexively, gauging his reply from my voice. It chunked into the metal just below my cheek.

Damn close!

I said, "I don't want to *have* to kill you," and put one between his feet.

He got the message and, reluctantly, let go of his gun.

"Back up."

He stepped back.

I moved over and kicked his gun into a corner.

"Your eyes will clear up in a few minutes," I said. "It would help if you rinsed them with water, though. You have any?"

"Yes."

There was a storage rack in a tiny grotto that contained a lavatory. I rinsed out a cloth and put it over his eyes. Then I took him by the arm and led him to the table. He slumped there while I went over and examined the canister item more closely.

I pounded it with my fist. "What is it?" I asked.

"It's the end of a pipeline," Skeeter John said without inflection.

"Oh?"

He gave a short nod. "About sixty years ago they used to unload tankers at a floating depot just off Isle Au Haut. There was a pipeline linking Isle Au Haut to the mainland."

"And this ties into that pipeline?"

"Yes. The tankers stopped delivering about thirty-five, forty years ago. Everyone just assumed the pipeline was shut down."

I whistled. "So okay. You have a pipeline that runs from Bar Harbor to Isle Au Haut. That's what, eighty, ninety miles?"

"It's not *on* Isle Au Haut," he said. "That would've been too shallow for the tankers. It's ten miles or so to the south, in open water."

"I see. And what do you do with it?"

For the first time he gave a little chuckle.

"Emeralds."

I stopped wondering how he had gotten rich.

I asked him how it worked and he told me. There were certain ships, with South American registry, that stopped off Isle Au Haut before carrying their cargoes of bauxite and coffee into New York's harbors. The uncut emeralds were put into a compressed rubber "pig" the size of a cannonball and dropped into the depot end of the pipeline. There was an automatic pumping station there that provided necessary line pressure, and the emeralds ended their Pan-American tour in Skeeter John's rubber-lined catcher's mitt—an eighty-mile line drive.

"My generating station lowers air pressure in the pipeline," Skeeter John finished. He shrugged then and laughed, the sound quickly dying out. "I meant what I said earlier—ten percent of the take if you come in with me."

I thought it over. After each delivery Skeeter John dropped the emeralds off to a certain party who paid cash and asked no questions. After sending part of the profit back to South America, he could spend his lonely evenings counting hundred-dollar bills.

"Who are Georgie and Fricci?"

"Georgie is muscle. Leonard Fricci likes to freelance in the gem trade."

"Freelance—like stealing you blind and beating you up?"

"Yeah," he said. "That kind of freelance."

I said, "How do your eyes feel?"

He took away the cloth. "Better. I can see something besides blue stars. What did you do, anyway?"

"It was just a pinch of flash powder," I said. "I got lucky. And, by the way, I'm not with the competition, whoever they might be."

He nodded. "That's why I suggested a partnership." He paused for a second and then said, "Thanks for saving my life—twice." He managed a grin in my direction and then collapsed across the table. He was tough, but the men who'd beaten him up were tougher.

I got him over to the elevator-closet and from there, eventually, back into bed. Rest was what he needed now—more than medicine, more even than a doctor.

Dawn was not far away, and the wind had quieted. I went down to my cottage, the fourth in an unlovely line of twelve. I took off my clothes, climbed into the shower, and adjusted its rusted head to needle-spray. It helped; the throbbing ache in my leg began to abate.

After dressing again, I slogged through the slush to the road and followed that around to the big house on the point. It was instant gothic, with gingerbread relief, high spires, and waves that pounded against black granite forty feet below.

There'd been money spent on it, but only enough to forestall imminent decay. Inside, though, it was furnished comfortably in tweeds and leathers. There was a library full of books, and paintings, some of them well done, of old clippers and steam packets. The floors were carpeted in earth tones, greens and browns.

There was a fireplace in one of the drawing rooms that drew my eye. It was flanked by caddies of kindling wood and nested bronze fire irons. Above it on the mantel were a variety of clocks and barometers. There was a calendar there, too, a date on it circled in red. It was the first day of May, one year earlier.

Reunion day. A day when the Gods would come calling . . . well, one of them, anyway.

I had never cared much for reunions. . . .

Chapter Fourteen

Rest Skeeter John needed, and rest he got. I covered for him on the pipeline and took in one small shipment, a handful of dirty, sharp-edged pebbles. I spread them out on the table and looked at them, trying to imagine them cut and polished and glowing with green light. I tried to imagine them in a necklace around Catherine's neck. Then I smoked a cigarette and put them in a chamois bag and took them upstairs to Skeeter John.

He stayed in bed a week, the bruises fading from purple to blue-green. Then he exercised, working out three days a week, taking long walks in the snow.

When he was ready, we rolled. I rode shotgun, and we delivered three more shipments of emeralds before the competition decided to have another go at us.

They picked their place well, a part of the highway that narrowed and bent back upon itself. The top of the resulting U dropped precipitously thirty feet into the Penobscot, a churning muddy channel filled with melte.

We came over a rise and saw the roadblock immediately. They had turned a truck broadside, jackknifing the cab, giving us only about two feet on either side.

Flares lit up the dark, making flickering eerie shadows that reached out at us like fingers.

"Hang on!" Skeeter John yelped. He clamped his jaw tight, narrowed his eyes. His hands tightened on the yoke. The little electric slewed sideways, rocking heavily on its suspension. Then the seat belt was digging into my midriff and the cone of our lights danced crazy patterns in the air. In the space of one insane moment we had switched end for end and were headed back the other way. I heard the engine whining pitifully, a muttered curse I knew to be my own, and then we were into another headlong slide.

They had anticipated us, blocked our retreat with a panel truck. We did the end-swap thing again, showering gravel out into space, nearly following it out there ourselves. There was still nobody in sight, though the shadows would hide an army.

We saw them when we bore down upon the truck again. Three men, startled at our quick maneuvering. Two of them had handguns, one what looked to be a shotgun. They knelt and fired and the windshield starred suddenly.

I snapped a shot at the man with the shotgun and another at a man diving back behind the truck.

Then Skeeter John suddenly laughed his old open-throated laugh and his foot came down hard on the accelerator.

"What is it?"

He said, "Find something and hang on!"

He'd spotted a ramp of loose stone that led up onto the apron of the wall, the inner portion of the U. We hit it at top speed and tilted up and sideways. Our speed carried us perhaps twenty feet beyond the bulk of the truck.

We continued on for a quarter of a mile, then Skeeter John snapped off the lights, turned the car around, and parked.

"We're going back," he said, his voice deceptively neutral.

I allowed a moment to recover. Then I shrugged. "That follows," I told him.

We climbed out of the electric and were swallowed up by the night. We ran, Skeeter John a half step ahead, the sound of his shoes on asphalt soft and quick.

And just like that, it took me back. I was in the army, in battle gear and camouflage. Ahead the horizon's skirts were rucked by flashes of green and white. Mark was a dim shape on my left and . . .

I shook my head and exorcised that particular demon. Mark was dead; I had killed him.

"You go left," Skeeter John murmured over his shoulder. "I'll take the right."

"Yo."

I ran, and my leg ached.

They were fools—they had no lookouts, and they were all four crouched in the light of the flares. One of them, the one who had had the shotgun, was moaning and coughing blood.

I edged around the truck's cab, keeping in shadow, waiting for Skeeter John to get set.

Then I heard him, and he was laughing.

"All right, clowns," he said. "Just freeze where you are."

They didn't, of course. Two of them broke away, rolling for the edge of the roadway. Skeeter John shot them both.

The other man lifted the fallen shotgun, and I fired before he could get it to his shoulder. He slumped down across the other man and did not move.

We buried them where they might have buried us, in the all-concealing waters of the Penobscot. The trucks we moved farther down the road, parking them at the nearest wide space.

Later, sitting in the electric, our cigarettes white holes in the darkness, we listened to the enveloping hush.

"I guess you'll sleep better, now," I said. I gave him a grin.

He gave me a glance and then an answering grin. "That's right," he said. "I will."

After a few minutes we flipped the cigarettes out the window and drove north to deliver the shipment.

Chapter Fifteen

Danelon moved his rook and I saw trouble ahead. He was already up a tempo, and he had earlier pinned a knight. His queen bishop, fianchettoed, bore squarely down on my center pawn—and now his rook backed it up.

I took a sip of beer.

"Reunion day, hmm?" Danelon inquired.

I nodded.

"You aren't sticking around for it?"

I shook my head. "I'm finishing this beer and this game and then I'm leaving. I don't like the Harbor, Frank. Too cold, too wet."

I took another sip, and remembered how it had gone.

The first to show up were Elizabeth and George Foster, with their three children. They arrived three days before the reunion and stayed in the big house on the point.

The following day came Edward and Alice Branham, Roberta Jocasta Branham, and Edna Fitzpatrick Branham. Roberta and Edna were spinsters, one from Oregon,

143

one from Iowa. Edward and Alice had twin girls twelve years old.

The day before the reunion John Gage Branham showed up, a nineteen-year-old dropout who lugged a guitar and talked with a nasal twang.

The last to arrive was Christopher Bishop Branham, a near-hermit who ran a homestead on the other side of the Canadian line.

Thirteen of them altogether; brother, sister, uncle, aunt. A significant number: an omen.

The evening before the reunion, the last solemn day of April, everyone met at the big house for drinks.

I, dressed in white dinner jacket and black tie, served as co-host.

"This is Scott Chesbro," Skeeter John said. "He's my friend and partner." He turned and looked at me and his blue eyes lighted.

I grinned at him and grinned at his guests. I was no longer Scott Chesbro, though. I was instead Sisyphus—strong, dark-minded Sisyphus.

"Welcome to Bar Harbor," I said. "You're harbingers of Spring, you know. May birds. Let's drink a toast to that." And I walked across the room to where the liquor cabinet stood.

"Do you know what they're doing *now*?" Alice Branham asked.

"The Triumvirate?" I shook my head. "We always get the news late, here on the point."

She was a big woman, with frosted champagne hair and inquisitive green eyes. She wore a string of matched pearls and a dress the color of new cream. She had a fine, even, *cafe au lait* tan. She reminded me of women who had attended Warmath's parties—brilliant, polished, radiating allure through every line of cloth and curve. I pitied Edward and at the same time wanted to drag his wife off and jump on her bones.

"They're building a temple," she said. "Somewhere out in Idaho or Utah. It's going to be a shrine bigger than the pyramids."

We moved out onto a balcony. Below us a heavy surf drummed against the cliffs. It was cold yet, and there was a wind blowing. Alice Branham shivered but did not go back inside.

"I'm frightened," she said after a time. "Terrified, if you want to know the truth."

I took a long sip of Scotch and stared over her shoulder at the stars in the eastern sky. I shrugged. Who wasn't frightened these days?

"What will they do, I wonder? How far will they go? I don't want the twins to grow up in a world like this."

"Even gods can't live forever," I said lightly, with some prophecy. I wondered why she had chosen me to talk to thus.

"Skeeter thinks very highly of you," she said as if in answer. "And you make me feel comfortable. You won't report my treason, will you?" She gave me a quick smile, then leaned against the railing. The wind fluttered, then flattened the dress against her body. It revealed everything but her frame of mind.

"Oh, there you are," Edward Branham said. He gave me a look of icy territoriality and slipped a stole about his wife's bare shoulders.

I left them and refilled my glass with Scotch.

"Having fun?" Christopher Branham asked. He seemed amused. He had eyes as blue as Skeeter John's.

I gave a noncommittal answer.

"Skeeter John says you made up some games for us tomorrow."

"He asked me to," I said. "You always play games on reunion day?"

Christopher cocked his head to one side and shot me a look. He chuckled.

"Getting a mite old, myself, but yes, we've always

had games on reunion day. The kids enjoy them—and not only the young ones, either. What've you lined up for us?"

I shrugged, then lifted my gaze to study the room. The Branhams were a fine clan, I thought; they made a nice bell curve. On one hand there was Alice, sensual and cultured and ripe as a Georgia peach. On the other hand there was Jon Gage Branham, with his five-string guitar. He hadn't washed in at least a week and he had a stash of reefers inside his boot-top. I'd made it a point to keep upwind of him. Somewhere in the middle of the curve were the spinster sisters, with their white hair and faces stolen off old calendars. Where Skeeter John fit in I didn't know. Then it came to me. He was the black sheep, the disreputable relative the others secretly cherished.

"Oh," I said to Old Christopher, "I thought up a couple you should find interesting. I can't tell you, though. That would spoil the fun."

I mingled, and drifted, and at midnight I left the revel. I wandered along the cliff top. Far out on the water a light dipped and winked, a buoy marking the outward channel. There were sounds too, low-range organlike echoes that murmured and boomed with sullen intensity.

I sat on an out-thrusting jut of granite and sipped Scotch.

Games, I thought. Games . . .

One I had devised was simple enough. A scavenger hunt that took the participants to the far corners of the point. Each one would receive a sealed envelope with map and instructions. The first to return with his list complete was the winner.

Out on the water there was a splash, and then the satisfied cry of a night bird, a harsh sound that reverberated along the line of cliffs. Another hunter, I thought with wry amusement, another predator both invisible and deadly: welcome, brother.

I grinned in the darkness then, and turned away, heading back toward the house.

"Where will you go now?" Danelon asked. He watched me move a pawn and immediately punished me by advancing one of his own.

"West," I said. "Or maybe south. Arizona sounds nice."

He shook his head sadly.

"I couldn't travel like that anymore. I'd miss the ocean, the smell and feel of it. You stay here long enough, it gets in your blood."

"That's what I'm afraid of," I said. I grinned at him and then looked at the Bavarian cuckoo clock over the bar. Eleven o'clock. Out on the point they would be opening their envelopes, getting ready for the hunt.

One of those envelopes directed its recipient to the closet-elevator in Skeeter John's cottage. It said to pick up a green stone from a table in a hidden room.

It did not, however, say anything about a fail-safe, or about a bomb put there to help it along.

I finished my beer and grinned again at Danelon. They would have to think up another name now, I thought. It wouldn't be a triumvirate any longer.

Besides, Jon Gage never *could* play the guitar.

Games . . .

"The game is over," I said to Danelon. Then I rose to my feet and walked out the door. I never looked back.

Chapter Sixteen

It was evening. New Mexico, not Arizona. Outside my hotel room the city dwelt in shadow. I opened a window and looked down, finding finally the ribbon of concrete that ran across the plaza. The air flowing over me was warm, off the desert, and I welcomed it as a thirsty man welcomes drink.

I moved to the bed and sat down. With my back against a pillow, and my feet hung out over the edge of the mattress, I could just make out the terrace apartment belonging to Charles L. Heywood.

He was an important man, a member of the mayor's select committee, one of the wealthiest citizens in the city. Now I sat and watched the square of light that darkened occasionally with his angular shadow. And I wondered how I could tempt his brother down from Up-Top so that I could kill him.

In the morning I showered and brushed my teeth and looked out the window again. I was waiting for Heywood to go to work. Often, I accompanied him.

While I waited I let my eyes rove over the mutated jacaranda trees lining the walks. In the early morning

149

light their limbs made tangled shadows against the concrete. Nightmare shapes. Sometimes the architects get carried away with their ability to mold, to change. Different, after all, is not always better. I would have preferred stately oaks to the monstrous monkey bars I saw below.

A little after nine Heywood left his apartment and drove downtown to the Municipal Building. I followed him in a taxi. I watched him ease his electric into the parking garage and hand over his keys to an attendant. Then he turned left and wove his way through the rivers of pedestrians to the entrance of the office complex. He was an easy man to follow—he towered half a head above those around him, and he was wearing the black and silver uniform that designated his office.

I didn't follow him into the building. There were cameras set up all around the entrance, and inside there was a policeman checking identification.

I doubted they would recognize me; I was becoming very good at changing faces—Sam would have been proud of me. But there *was* such a thing as tempting fate.

I crossed the street, bought a newspaper from a blind vendor. He was wearing a medal from one of the African campaigns. More personnel in the field, I thought grimly. I overtipped him and recrossed the street to a snack bar half-filled with secretaries and office workers.

Over coffee and toast I reacquainted myself with the state of the world.

Item: The shrine in southern Utah was nearly finished. It was over a thousand feet high, cut from marble the Gods had brought from Italy.

Item: A tactical nuclear weapon had been exploded in Africa, destroying half of Fanny VI's dormant copters. The nuclear device was brought in by what amounted to a group of kamikaze saboteurs.

And, as if in retaliation . . .

Item: Forty members of a Brazilian underground had been found and executed.

Item: Over ten percent of the Sahara had been reclaimed for agricultural purposes.

There was nothing about the incident in Bar Harbor. Nothing new, that is. The day after it happened there had been a single report confirming the cave-in, then a total blackout of news from the area.

There had been one other bulletin, though. Local officials were looking for a man calling himself Scott Chesbro. They wanted him on a charge of grand theft.

I grinned into my coffee cup. Perhaps even gods could be frightened.

Outside on the sidewalk I shaded my eyes and looked up at the sixteenth floor of the Municipal Building. Heywood's office. Perhaps I would find the answer I sought there, when I visited it later that night.

You can have your full moon, with its pocked and cratered face. It makes lunatics, after all, and rightly named.

I crouched where the shadows were darkest and cursed the wan white light. On the street beyond a police car slowed, its occupants peering uncertainly at the darkened stairwells. I crouched and waited and, satisfied at last, they moved on.

There would be sensors inside the building—too many and too well hidden for me to avoid them all.

I stared instead at the vertical cliff of the building's southern wall. It was one hundred sixty feet to Heywood's office. The high road. I slipped on a camouflage coat, palmed two magnetic discs, slapped them hard against the cold surface.

Cursing the moonlight, I climbed.

I made it without hearing a challenge from below, though my back itched and I felt vulnerable and exposed hanging on the side of the building.

The office window was closed and sealed, but there were ways around that. It took two minutes, and then I had the window up and myself inside. I paused to look down, at the rivers of concrete that flowed through metal canyons. There were no police cars in sight. I grinned then at the lunatic moon and drew the drapes.

Heywood's office was sparsely furnished, with clean lines predominating. There were good charcoals on the walls, a few chairs, a coffee table, half an acre of deep green carpet, and a desk that could have fielded a polo team. I sat down in Heywood's leather captain's chair, turned on a gooseneck lamp, and went methodically through the desk drawers. There was nothing of interest except a loaded pistol. I left it where it was and studied the room carefully. Heywood would have a safe somewhere close.

I started taking down a picture, then stopped, my ears catching a slight scraping sound. Sudden adrenalin made my muscles tense, set my heart pounding.

I stood there without moving. I listened, thought.

I heard the scrape again.

Then the office was flooded with light. Two men came through the door in a rush, their weapons snapping up, their eyes widening when they saw me.

"Hold it right there!"

I stood without moving, the picture held in nerveless fingers.

"Who are you?" one of them asked.

"Stewart Jackson," I said. There was identification on me. My present alias.

"Turn around slowly, Mr. Jackson," the other man said. He grinned at me, not pleasantly. He was big, with a scar that drew down one side of his mouth.

They were dressed in green security uniforms, so they weren't police. That much went on my side of the ledger. They looked competent, though, and there was something professional about the one with the scar. I decided I did not want to stick around to answer questions.

I looked at them, smiled disarmingly.

Then I went into set.

Sisyphus . . .

More of the polylux exploding, clouds of pepper aureoling their heads, a rain of small stones thudding off their helmets. I laughed softly, eased away from the wall, went out the door. I locked it behind me—it had been easy.

Too easy.

Something clamped my arm in an iron vise. I felt myself lifted, thrown upward by a force I could not resist. I slammed hard against the ceiling, bounced off. Stars flashed across my vision.

I heard a dull booming sound, and recognized it after a moment. Celestial laughter. Divine mirth. The mutterings of a mad Zeus.

I fought. I shattered the lights with a hail of lead pellets. I grappled in darkness against mad genie fingers. Almost, I got away. Then I was lifted again, hurled against a wall. The mutterings grew louder, then subsided. The dark grew velvety and soft, drowning me. I felt myself being lifted again, hurled again. The darkness grew softer still. Finally, it grew total.

When I woke up, it was to the harsh searing stab of overhead lights. I blinked, pushed against some sort of harness that secured me to a bed.

"He's awake," a voice said. It came from my left, in the shadows beyond my vision.

"Turn on the machine," somebody else said. It was a harsh jarring voice I recognized immediately.

"Sandone?"

"You've given me a lot of trouble," Sandone said. "Now shut up!" He sounded in a rage, as if he'd been chewing barbed wire.

I started to speak anyway, but was interrupted by a buzzing sound that came from something strapped around my head. I closed my eyes against the pain, then opened them again.

Sandone came into view, bent down over me, his searchlight stare as cold and distant as ever. He touched a control on a small boxlike affair and the buzzing grew fainter, but did not go away.

"That's to stop you from using the sets," he explained waspishly. He thumbed my head with a stubby forefinger. "And now it's time to find out just what it is I created inside there."

"Where am I?" I asked. "The Municipal Building?"

"No. My old laboratory. I opened it up again; you're in Pittsburgh." He stared at me, his face owlish and round and suffused with anger.

So I was back home again.

"How did you find me?" I asked.

Sandone snorted. "We aren't idiots, you know. Especially after what happened at Bar Harbor. We took precautions."

They had been waiting for me. I gave myself a mental kick for underestimating the opposition.

"How do you do it?" Sandone asked next.

"Do what?"

He sighed. "Let's start with the stones and lead pellets we found in the Municipal Building. And the polylux. It *was* polylux, wasn't it?"

"Yes."

"All right. How did you do it?"

I shrugged. "I don't know."

"Don't know? Or won't tell?"

I raised an eyebrow. "Call it a knack."

He gave me a scowl, then looked beyond me at his invisible helper.

"Give me a hypo."

A hand came into view and handed him the instrument.

"Anything else to say?"

"No."

I felt the needle's sting then, and once more I started that long slide that had always ended in the inner labyrinths of my mind.

There were a few familiar boundaries. Landmarks. I knew I had been this way before.

There were differences too, of course. The friendly chirruping sounds were gone, in their place a too-rapid tinny drumming. It was loud, and not so friendly.

There was a man there, sitting on a horse. He gave me a lugubrious smile and came closer. No man. No horse. Chiron the physician, struck alive by the whisper of God.

"You're in big trouble now, friend."

"I know. You come to help?"

"Maybe. If you hop up here on my back I'll take you away from here. This world stretches out forever, you know. There are lots of places to hide—if you have that in mind."

"You know some good places?"

"Some dandy ones."

"Places where even Sandone can't find me?"

There was a brazen grin.

I was silent for a moment, listening to the tinny discord. I thought about a lot of things as I shared space with this relic of myths. Finally, though, I made up my mind. I gave him a smile.

"I appreciate the offer, but I don't think hiding is the answer. Keep me in mind, though, huh?"

He tilted his head to one side. "It's going to get worse before it gets better, you know. In fact, it may not *get* better."

"You're a pillar of strength."

"Don't be droll. It occurs to me that if you go, I go too."

"You've got a point," I said. I looked at him more

closely, and, almost, stepped forward to join him. But I stayed myself, and the impulse passed.

He sensed the nuance of the moment and gave me a lopsided mocking smile. Then he composed his features and folded his arms. He gave a small shrug.

"It was nice knowing you," he said.

"I'll see you again."

"Don't bet on it."

Somebody was playing with the light, turning it alternately gray and green. The tin drum began a palsied, inarticulate rhythm. Parts of Chiron began to disappear.

"Your master seeks your attention, Sisyphus."

"He's no master of mine."

"He is, though. And your destiny."

I looked after him as he vanished into shadow. Then I felt Sandone's gentle touch, knocking on the door of my awareness; knocking with brass knuckles.

I opened my eyes, stared into the overheads. The band around my head made spitting sounds. I hurt, and I suspected the centaur physician was right. It was going to get worse before it got better.

Off to my left there was sudden movement. I rotated my head enough to see.

"I can find out what I want to know," Sandone said gratingly. "Even if you fight me. You know me—you know that to be true. I suggest you *don't* fight me. The long result of that would be to have your brain turned into tapioca."

"You mean you care?" I asked sardonically.

He snorted. "Of course I care. You're invaluable, unique. I would hate to destroy you, Gilliam."

"But you would."

"If you don't cooperate." He paused. "You remember Toby, don't you? He's recovering very nicely, no thanks to you. You didn't do any permanent damage. Unfortunately, those same techniques would not work with you. I would have to go deeper, perhaps into the psyche itself. If I had to do that there would be very little of you left."

He stopped talking and we regarded one another. Two enemies fencing. Only one had a foil.

"And if I do cooperate?" I asked.

"We'll see. Heywood and Morse wanted you dead—they think you're too dangerous. But I think you could be a valuable addition to our group. I might convince them if I tried."

I wondered what kind of god I would make. Would I help Man transcend his humble condition, or would I lead him into Hell?

This asked of Sisyphus, who toils upon that mountain in Hades' own domain.

I looked at Sandone.

"I'll cooperate," I said.

He looked surprised, then in order, pleased and cynical.

"I'm sure you will. Tell me, for instance, how your particular talent works."

"I honestly don't know. I use the sets, then push—and things disappear. Small things. Where they go I don't know. I pull, and they reappear. Turn this headband off and I'll show you."

He took off his glasses, polished them, and then put them back.

"Tell me about the underground."

"I don't know anything to tell."

"You mean they haven't been hiding you, supporting you?" He looked disbelieving.

"That's what I mean."

He shook his head. "You'll have to do better than that. Is Warmath a member?"

"A member of what?"

"The underground."

"No."

"And the girl, Catherine Delaney?"

"No. But then you would know better than I. You've had them both under surveillance since Fannon's death."

Sandone did not say anything, but his expression gave him away. He and the gods had been using them for bait.

"It was your idea alone to kill Avery Fannon and Chester Markham?"

"It was my idea to kill Fannon," I corrected. "Mark's death was an accident."

Sandone started to pace. After a moment he stopped and put his hands in his trouser pockets, then took them out again. He leaned over me, glaring.

He clenched his jaw and snapped, "I'm going to take you apart, Warren. I'm going to open you up like an oyster. And somewhere in there, I'll find out what I want to know."

"I told you I'd cooperate."

"Hah! Too late. Your cooperation is of no importance any more." He gestured for a hypo, held it in his hand inches from my arm. Just before he made the injection he leaned close and his eyes met mine.

"Chester Markham was your brother," he said. Then, savagely, "Avery Fannon was mine."

It is amazing what impetus can do for nightmare. Chili sauce and delicatessen dills had always done it for me as a child, and, later on, the memory of shells screaming overhead, the salty taste of my own blood.

Those were as nothing. Now there was Sandone. He came into my mind and sat there like a gluttonous vulture.

Down there in the labyrinth, the landscape was sere, full of gray plain and broken black stone. The sky was an ugly yellow, and the sounds were all lonely, echoes of echoes.

Though I tried, I could not move. I was trapped in

that seeming helpless state of dreams, where limbs do not obey will.

Something drifted past me, something that began to blaze with soft light. It grew, took on form.

"Mark?" I heard myself say.

He looked at me sadly, eyes hooded, yellow hair lying wetly on his skull.

"I'm going away, Gil," he said. "And this time my death will be the true one."

"What—"

"Don't talk. There's nothing you can say." He paused and shook his head. "In the true death even your memories of me will die."

I looked then and the light was gone. So too was . . . something . . . someone . . . I hadn't wanted to lose. Something wet scalded my eyes and I wished I could remember.

There was more movement. Other lights came into view, dancing their way across the stones. As they came closer, I cried out, for I knew what Sandone was doing.

They came and went, like phantoms, blazing into extinction in the air above the plains. Memories. People. Pieces of my life.

Alex . . . Sam . . .

"Craft," a voice said, and I wondered who that was, though I saw a wide stretch of beach and the white shine of a death-clock.

"Skeeter John," the voice whispered, and I felt the blows of a winter's wind.

"Julius Warmath," the same voice murmured. I caught a glimpse of brassy fire.

"Catherine Delaney," said the gloating voice, and I watched the blazing light and felt the pang of loss.

The voice went on and on. With each bursting light I grew more diminished.

I remembered a dream I had had, where Sandone walked about a mandala, half Sandone, half Fannon.

Had that been an esper's flash of precognition, a warning of danger soon to come?

Then that memory, too, was gone.

I stood alone at the edge of eternity. I watched the sky darken from mustard to dull rose to dirty gray. As night came on I wiped the spittle from my chin and wished the voice would stop.

Book Two

Chapter Seventeen

There were mountains, but not people. There were sunlit beaches full of empty footprints. There were unbroken horizons, and harsh winter snows that filled the land.

Bleak and empty and beset by impotence, I stared up at the cloud-blown sky.

And wept.

Alone I was—for all eternity. . . .

"Bastard! Wake up!" I got a hard shove in the ribs. From a week's worth of memory I rolled over, out of reach, and stared up at my attacker.

She had the deep-sunken eyes of the starving, though God knows she got enough to eat. From the waist up she was a loose bag of sticks, from the waist down a pocket half-track. She was, literally, hell on wheels.

Her name was Jessica Dos Santos. A fine old name, though I wondered how many of the generic Dos Santos' would claim this mad witch as one of their own.

Around me, the other shonzos stirred, their thin arms and legs a dull unhealthy white. The one nearest to me, a pathetic creature named Tidman, moved too slowly. He received a cane across his ribcage that doubled him up and left him gasping.

"Bastard!" murmured the witch, and wheeled away into her quarters.

I looked at the others. The man, Dickson, might have been a military man at one time; his carriage still possessed a certain stiffness. To his left was Tidman, still gasping, his face a mottled blue. Beyond them both was the one named Tuttle. He had a waxy complexion, grizzled black hair, and brown liquid eyes. Intelligent eyes. Ancient eyes.

He gave me a faint grin of recognition as he climbed to his feet. More a grimace, really, than a grin. It was Tuttle who had found me—and dragged me back to work for Jessica the Mad.

Someday I'll pay him back for that.

He had found me in one of the garbage pits down by the river, already half-buried in slime. I looked, later. There was an eight-foot fence there, and several pairs of footprints attesting to a monumental *alley-oop*.

My first remembrance was of Jessica, her eyes green-flecked and bright, her mouth drawn into a lipless snarl.

"What's your name?" she'd asked savagely.

I had looked at her, at Tuttle standing beside her. I thought about it. It was, indeed, an interesting question. Finally, I shook my head. I felt odd, my mind dismembered.

"Don't know," I said, croaking. "I can't remember."

She wheeled her chair closer and poked me with the business end of a steel cane.

"Try!"

So I tried, without much success, to remember what had happened to me before Tuttle fished me out of the slime. It was no use; things stayed foggy. Sweat stung my eyes. Then knives began to work inside my head and my knees turned to jelly.

"*. . . oh god . . . oh god!*"

"Try!" Jessica ordered again.

I did, and there was a Niagara of pain, an agony that went on and on, engulfing me. I stopped thinking and started screaming.

Tuttle picked me up off the floor sometime later and dumped me back into the chair I'd fallen out of. He was stronger than he first appeared.

"Somebody doesn't love you overmuch," Jessica said judicially. She raised an eyebrow. "You've had your cerebrum massaged, is what."

"Cere—what?"

She gave me a glance. "It's a thing they do—to traitors and squealers and quislings. A mind-rub. Most not as much as you, though . . . I wonder what you did."

I wondered too, but carefully, so as to not start the knives working again.

"Who's *they*?" I asked instead. I looked around. The walls had stopped swaying and the light fixtures had settled back into the ceiling where they belonged.

"Who are *they*?" Jessica ground out the question. "The underground, maybe—or the authorities. Someone with power—mind-rubbing is expensive." She stared at me with near hatred.

There was a short silence, then she inched her wheelchair forward until her face was about a foot from mine. A vein pulsed beneath the pale flesh of her cheek.

"They did a good editing job on you, that's for sure. Don't you remember *anything*?"

I gave it a minute, then shook my head.

A furrow etched itself between her brows and her eyes narrowed.

"If you're police, I'll chop you into small pieces, so help me!"

She meant it; she looked capable of mayhem.

After a moment she leaned her head to one side and backed away.

"What do you think, Tuttle?"

Tuttle's voice was crisp, precise, measured.

"He's not police."

"What makes you so sure?"

"His leg is full of shrapnel. He's an army veteran; he would never pass a police physical."

Jessica pondered that and then looked at me. "Are you hungry?"

I said I was.

She disappeared into another room and came rolling out presently with a pitcher of milk, half a loaf of bread, and a plate of cold stew. It was filling, but it would never win blue ribbons. I ate and they watched, and when I was halfway through, two more men came in. They sat down in the dim area beyond the circle of light and waited patiently to be fed. Tidman and Dickson, I learned later, coming home to mamma spider.

When I finished the stew Tuttle passed me a cigarette. I welcomed the tobacco's harshness, the comforting taste. While I smoked I pondered the four of them, and let my eyes rove around the cellar.

It was evening outside. It had begun to rain, and water rushed in the gutters. The shadows in the cellar were kept at bay by two dimly glowing overheads. I smelled the moisture, and noted how every sound seemed magnified. I smoked my cigarette down to a stub and crushed it out against the concrete.

"You need rest," Jessica said abruptly. She sounded angry, still. Angry and resigned. She went to a low cabinet and pulled a blanket out of a drawer. "You can sleep over there," she said, and pointed to an alcove beneath the stairs.

I bedded down in a bunk alongside the little man, Tidman, who fell asleep immediately, his blanket drawn

up to his chin. Beyond him were two other mounds—
Dickson and Tuttle. Where Jessica had gone I had no
idea. She had simply disappeared at some point into
one of the connecting rooms.

Tidman was snoring and the air smelled of night rain.
I tried, but I was suddenly so tired that it was impossible to think coherently. I lay in the darkness and listened to the others and thought about the slime pits.
Finally, imperceptibly, I fell asleep.

And wept.

And dreamed of wastelands and unnamed ghosts.

The breakfast next morning was uninspired, the company reminiscent of an asylum's back wards. Jessica
rolled in and out of the room with food, and the three
shonzos watched her with enigmatic eyes.

When the meal was over there was no time spent in
idle chat. Jessica came around the table and touched
me with the end of her cane.

"You, Jack. You'll go with Tuttle."

"Jack?"

"It's as good a name as any, isn't it? You have a
preference?"

"No. Jack will do."

"Well, then. Get going!" She raised her cane and
glared at us all. Her eyes were bitter, filled with hidden
pain.

Outside the cellar, Dickson and Tidman went west,
their pairing a wordless thing, an act of long standing.
Tuttle sniffed at the air and then took my arm.

"Foraging time," he said without emotion. "We find
food or we don't eat." He pointed east, toward a forest
of medium-sized gray buildings.

As we approached the first edifice it began to rain
again. The concrete alleyways glistened. I breathed
deeply, and watched water rivulet down broken win-
dowpanes. It was time I found out a few things.

"Listen," I said to Tuttle's back. "I'd appreciate some answers. Who the hell is Jessica? And what are you and she and the others doing here?"

Tuttle paid no attention to me. He paused after a moment and looked around. Then he consulted some inner map and spent time pondering coordinates. Finally, he made his decision.

"This way," he said. He gestured at an access route that wound between two buildings.

I followed, angrily. and banged my foot on a *punji* trap of rusted pipe. Tuttle looked back briefly and grinned at my curses. He was armed, I noticed. There was the butt of a pistol sticking out of his belt.

"What happened?" I asked. "Why are these buildings empty?"

There was no answer. We searched for two hours.

Then Tuttle grunted something, stopped, peered upward at a grillwork that opened out into the access space.

"Give me a leg up."

I formed my hands into a stirrup and lifted him up to the grill. After a moment or two he grunted again, this time in a more satisfied tone. He began to work on the grill.

"You've brought good luck," he said, peering down at me. "This looks like a storehouse."

Just before my arms tired beyond bearing, he levered the grill free of its moorings and pushed it through into the building. Then he gripped the edges of the hole and muscled himself through after it.

"Come on up," he said. He leaned out of the hole and extended his arm.

Inside, the storehouse was dimly lighted, the area in back of Tuttle filled with crates and baskets and what looked like bales of sacking. Tuttle went from row to row. He looked pleased.

He gave me a glance. "Over here, shonzo. Lend a hand."

I helped him open a crate. It was full of cans of sardines. He pried one open, tasted it, then looked up and grinned.

"It's still good. Cans last a long time."

I sat down on a crate and stared at him. "What's a shonzo, Tuttle? I want answers."

The other relaxed somewhat. Finding the storehouse had taken the edge off him. He fumbled in his shirt pocket for a cigarette, looked at me, fumbled yet again. He lit both cigarettes with a battered silver lighter.

"We're shonzos because we belong to Jessica Dos Santos," he said without inflection. "That simple enough?"

"Like slaves?"

"Yeah, like slaves. You too, now."

My fingers spasmed and the cigarette I'd been holding snapped against another crate. I looked at Tuttle for a long time before I leaned forward and picked it up.

"That's crazy! Who says we belong to her? I don't belong to anybody."

Tuttle shrugged and leaned back comfortably against the bales of sacking.

"I didn't say you had to believe it, Jack. None of us did—at first."

"But you believe it."

He nodded. "I *know* it."

"Tell me how."

He looked at me through a contrail of blue smoke. "You ever hear of the Medusa Project?"

"No."

"It was one of Avery Fannon's brainchildren, long before he got started in war computers."

I held up a hand and stopped him.

"Who is Avery Fannon?"

"Oh, sorry. I forgot." He grinned and gave me a quick rundown on Fannon.

"What does all that have to do with Jessica Dos Santos?" I asked when he was through.

He shrugged again and lit another cigarette. "She was one of the guinea pigs. And now she's the Medusa. One of Fannon's companies was involved in something they called Cathexis Theory. Ever hear of it?"

"No."

"Don't feel bad," Tuttle said. "Not many have. Anyway, Fannon came around a lot, talked with her, asked her questions. Later on, when the thing soured, he dumped her."

"What happened?"

The other man's smile was ironic. "They were almost *too* successful. The idea was to mold her into a super-spy, someone whose psi talent served as a locus for cathexes."

There was a moment of silence, and I broke it.

"What is she?" I asked. "A living voodoo doll?"

"Pretty close. Cathexis is psychic energy that demands attachment. Jessica generates a low-level field of that energy. She can't turn it off."

"Go on," I said.

He leaned back further, crossed one leg over the other. "You spend time close to her and the cathect sets in—like fishhooks. You can't leave her then, and you can't kill her." His face was a study of differing emotions. "In a strange way, you love her."

We stared at each other, and then he gave a metallic chuckle.

"You still don't believe me."

"No."

Tuttle put out his cigarette and climbed to his feet. "It doesn't matter if you believe me or not, Jack. You belong to Jessica Dos Santos, body and soul. We all do. Now help me with these crates."

He lifted two of the sardine containers and carried them over to the hole.

When we had a stack of six boxes I stepped back
warily and eyed the pistol in his belt.

"What would you do if I took some of this food and
just cleared out?"

He looked at me wearily, then grimaced. "Don't you
think the rest of us have tried? For God's sake, man—
you think we *like* living like this?"

"Then you won't stop me?"

He laughed out loud. "My friend, I won't stop you.
I'd go with you if I could."

I pointed to the buildings surrounding us. "Why are
they all abandoned?"

Tuttle shrugged and wriggled out of the hole. "This is
the Pittsburgh Plague Zone. They quarantined this whole
section of the city." He landed on bent legs and looked
up. "Toss down the boxes, shonzo. I've got to be getting back."

The rain had not stopped; it had instead intensified.
It fell straight down from leaden skies, overburdening
the gutters, washing in sheets across the concrete apron.
I watched Tuttle clear the mouth of the access route
and disappear from sight. His last glance back had been
a mocking one, that of a gambler who plays for the
house.

For fifteen minutes I walked toward the east. Then,
cold and wet, the streets still deserted before me, I
sought shelter beneath a green-shingled overhang. From
there I watched the rain and eyed the decaying buildings and picked over my thoughts like a carrion bird
picking over week-old bones.

Trying to think brought pain, though less this time
than last. It didn't get me anywhere, though, and after
a time I stopped and wrapped my hand in a handker-
chief, where I had been beating it against the wall.

The facts I had were few—and depressing. Someone
hated me enough to kill me. No. That needed correc-
tion. Someone hated me enough to mind-rub me and

throw me out like last week's garbage—an act that spoke more of contempt than murder.

Who would hate me thus?

I stood in silence and watched the rain, but that brought no inspiration. And after a while it occurred to me that even if I made it beyond the plague zone I had no idea what to do next. I had no money, no friends, and, worst of all, no plan.

I didn't like the conclusion, but I made it anyway.

As bad as it seemed, Jessica Dos Santos' cellar offered asylum until I could figure out my next step— until I could get my memory back.

Who *was* I? It was nerve-rattling to open the closet of my mind and find it picked clean. Well, no, it hadn't been picked entirely clean; there was evidence of hurried trespass. There was the casual land mine laid down to trap the unwary, the hacked and bloody feeling of someone bent on demolition.

The rain stopped, and I turned back the way I had come, suddenly aware of the silence, almost intimidating, and the bulky black squares that loomed on either side.

No one seemed surprised to see me. Dickson and Tidman gave me brief nods, and Tuttle greeted me with a wave of his hand. Jessica was nowhere in sight.

"The prodigal returns, I see," Tuttle said. The words were spoken flatly, without sarcasm.

"It's not what you think," I said. I looked past him. "And I won't be staying long—only until I get a few things settled in my mind."

Tuttle tapped out a cigarette, offered it to me, grinned.

"Me, too," he said.

"You think *she* brought me back?" I pointed toward the inner darkness.

He grinned a little more. "Well, the thought had crossed my mind. That low-level field of hers—it's pretty subtle at times. You probably thought you had valid reasons for returning."

I began an angry reply, then cut it off and stared at him.

"She can do that?"

Tuttle lit his own cigarette, looked at me, nodded.

And suddenly it hit me, like a physical blow. If Tuttle was right, it meant that Jessica, however unwittingly, was using our minds as weapons against themselves. Perhaps she was in truth a voodoo doll.

"Why didn't you tell me?" I asked.

"I tried to. Remember? It's not the kind of thing the average person believes without experiencing it firsthand." He moved over to the table and sat down. "You hungry?" he asked. "We've got plenty of sardines."

Chapter Eighteen

For the following two weeks we followed a strict routine. I grew used to the cane, used to the ignominy of a shadowy kind of half-life.

But, as yet, I had no memory. My past was unpeopled, a wasteland of information without source. Probably I had been a soldier. Tuttle said so, and I could see the marks of wounds upon my thigh, could feel the dull ache beneath the scars.

And sometimes when I dreamed I heard the wild shriek of shells, saw in their flash the pallid faces of fellow soldiers, nameless ghosts.

I was savant, but uncertain. And afraid.

Four times I tried to escape. Four times I came slinking back.

Outside the cellar, night lay like an ocean, surrounding our retreat, leaving it an island in an inkblot.

Dinner was thin soup and hard, crusty bread. Food was being rationed again; foraging was a sometime thing.

Jessica tapped me with her cane. There was something in her eyes. Not anger, this time—curiosity. She said, "Follow me," and wheeled through the arched doorway into her own quarters.

Tuttle gave me a startled look, but said nothing. I walked after her, forcing myself to stay calm. Never before had I been asked to her quarters.

The rooms she took me to were more brightly lighted than the main cellar. There were pictures on the walls and rugs on the floor. I looked at a jade vase full of silk flowers, knew somewhere she had robbed a museum.

She spun her wheelchair around and waited until I passed, then slammed the door. Oak, I guessed, from its long straight grain.

"Sit down," she said. "You'll find chairs just ahead and to your right."

I sat, and she stopped her wheelchair opposite me.

"You're wondering, I suppose, why I asked you in here."

"You could say that."

She put her hands in her lap, leaving the cane hooked over the arm of the chair.

"Perhaps you'd like to smoke."

"Yes, thanks."

"There on the table. Help yourself."

I opened a soapstone box, took out a cigarette, lit it with a gold lighter.

"I know who you are," Jessica said. She sat watching me, green eyes bright.

"Who?" She had taken me by surprise.

"Look at that newspaper," she said next. She grasped her cane and pointed at a half unfolded newsfax on one of the low tables. "Tidman brought it in earlier this evening. I don't think he even reads them anymore."

I picked it up. It was old, starting to fall apart along the creases. There was a picture on it, though—one I easily recognized. The text beneath it said: *Manhunt Over For Gil Warren. Assassin Dead*.

"Assassin? Me?" I stared at the paper in astonishment, then looked across at Jessica.

"Hardly a murderer, however," was her remark. She gave me a grim smile. "More a service for humanity."

I shook my head. "I don't understand. I never killed anybody."

"You killed Avery Fannon," Jessica said with satisfaction. "Blew him apart in spite of his 'divine protection.'" She laughed in a thin shrill voice and rolled forward a little, her eyes softening. "You want to know who did this to you? The Gods, is who! They wiped the slate clean, took their revenge."

I stared at her, not comprehending. She saw my look and laughed again.

"Over there on that sideboard you'll find some wine. Not good stuff, but the best I can do. Pour us each a glass. We'll toast the death of Avery Fannon—*may his soul rot!*"

Fannon. I recalled what Tuttle had said of him. I searched my memory, but found nothing.

Gilliam Warren. I ran the name over my tongue, but it had no familiarity. I poured the wine and resumed my seat.

"Nothing comes to you?"

"No."

We were silent for perhaps five seconds, then musingly, Jessica said, "I wonder what your Talent was."

I gazed at her over my glass. Her voice had lost its arrogant, commanding tone. She seemed almost happy.

"Talent?" I said. "What Talent?"

Jessica lifted her wine glass, stared at the rich ruby color. Then, sighing softly, she drank.

"You wouldn't know about Fannon," she said. "He exploited people, bought them and sold them. From contempt, probably." She paused for a second, studying the glass in her hand. Then she said bitterly, "He would have been wonderful in Auschwitz—!"

"You're saying he was a monster?"

"What else?" Her voice changed timbre. "He used *me*, made me the Medusa." She opened her mouth to say something more, closed it, ground her teeth together.

I said, "Tuttle told me a little about it. He said Fannon abandoned you when your affliction became permanent; he said it's the closest thing to an honest-to-god curse."

"It's hell!" Jessica exclaimed. Mouth twisted, she rocked in her chair. Wine from her glass spilled on the floor.

"And I killed the monster," I mused aloud. I looked at the paper again, at the likeness staring back at me. "You said I had a Talent. I wonder what it was." I sought within, found nothing to illuminate my quest.

Jessica caught my eye. "But you used it to kill him," she said. "He was protected, and you reached through all his defenses. You snuffed him out—like that!" She snapped her fingers. "Not only him, but the other one, too."

"The other one?"

She nodded. "Chester Markham. Another of the so-called gods."

There was nothing. I did not remember.

I finished my cigarette, and my wine, and we looked at each other.

"I don't know if there is a way to beat a mind-rub," Jessica said, her words clipped, run together. "Maybe, maybe not." She smiled suddenly, lopsidedly. "Not here, at any rate."

"Where, then?" I asked. "The outer city? A hospital?"

"No." She tapped her fingers idly on the steel shank of her cane. "Not a hospital. That would be reported, and sooner or later the Gods would know and hunt you down again. You're dead now. Better you stay dead."

I lit another cigarette, pondered a five-inch-high Etruscan warrior on the table before me. It was made from gold and showed exquisite craftsmanship. *Etruscan*. How could I have known that? Conversely, how could I not?

"You seem to be going out of your way to help me," I said finally. "That's not like you."

She laughed sharply, deeply. "You've done me a favor—killed Fannon. Besides, you're worth more to me if you can get your Talent back."

I gave her a mocking smile. "As a shonzo?"

Something flickered in her stare. "No. We're very much alike, you and I. More than you think. Now go away and let me think."

I put out my cigarette, stood up. I left her sitting in her chair in the middle of the room, her eyes looking without expression into her empty wine glass.

Tuttle looked at me questioningly when I returned, but I ignored him. I exited the cellar, walked slowly along the street. Above me stars gleamed, and the moon shone with a yellow light. I stopped, drew in a breath of cold night air.

Gilliam Warren. Though there were no memories, the feeling was still very good. An identity. Now I had something to call the face I saw in the mirror every morning.

Chapter Nineteen

At dawn, Jessica roused us.

"Eat your fill," she said. She had laid out tinned meat and biscuits, and hot black coffee. She watched us eat and said nothing. When we were finished she took away the dishes and came rolling to sit before us.

"Today we go to the Black Wall," she said. Her tone was deceptively mild, but her face was full of determination. She had dressed herself in clothes of nut brown and leaf green and there was a shotgun cradled in her lap.

Tidman and Dickson had stopped thinking long since. They merely reacted. They accepted Jessica's latest instructions with the blanked-out eyes of zombies.

Tuttle, however, looked up questioningly. He lit a cigarette and fingered his battered silver lighter. There was a pattern worked into the metal of a stag in flight. He rubbed it lightly with his thumb before speaking.

"The Wall is a couple of miles from here—beyond the Medusa field." He inhaled musingly. "That must be why you're going along. What's out there that's so interesting?"

"It's not what's there," Jessica said impatiently. "It's

what is on the other side. A clinic. It used to be run by a blacklisted surgeon named Victor Lorimar. Maybe it still is."

"We're going outside the Wall?" Tuttle's eyes narrowed. He seemed suddenly unsure of himself.

"*We're* not," Jessica said. "He is." She pointed in my direction with the end of her cane.

"He goes outside the Wall he'll die," Tuttle said bluntly. "Everybody knows that. He can't leave the Medusa field."

Jessica met bluntness with bluntness. "*You* can't, Tuttle. But he still has a chance."

Tuttle started to growl; Jessica silenced him. "Come on, all of you shonzos—let's go."

It had rained in the night and the streets were still damp, the moisture glistening in the bright sunlight. Tidman and Dickson were on point, Tuttle in the middle just in front of Jessica's wheelchair. I brought up the rear. I'd been told there were gangs that occasionally roamed through the plague zone. I had never seen them, but I *had* come across crushed cigarette butts and empty beer cans.

Some of the roadways were blocked, filled with rusted cars and fallen posts. We proceeded cautiously, picking our way through the debris. Once in a while we lifted Jessica over some of the larger obstacles. Overhead the sun grew bolder, and the concrete began to steam.

An hour later Jessica made an abrupt turn into an alley. "Stop here," she ordered curtly. The alleyway was full of tumbled bricks and rotted boards. Beyond the barrier was a steel spider web of scaffolding.

"What's wrong?" Tuttle asked. One hand rested lightly on the butt of his revolver.

"Nothing is wrong. The Wall is only a few blocks ahead." She turned to me and gave a tiny, humorless smile. "The Wall was built to keep vermin in, so the plague would not spread. It can easily be circumvented, however." She paused for a moment before continuing. "Follow this street; it ends at the Wall. There's a channel to your left, a tributary of the Allegheny River. Don't enter that channel—it's been electrified. Find another way across the Wall. Beyond it is Lorimar's clinic. Show him this." She removed the handle from her cane, took out a small piece of paper, and handed it to me. It bore four words: *By my hand. Medusa.*

"Let me go with him," Tuttle pleaded suddenly. His voice was unsteady, almost shrill.

"Stay here," Jessica commanded coldly. She raised her cane threateningly, then lowered it. An argument here would do none of them any good. She dismissed him with a glance, then gave me a ghost of a smile and pointed to the street.

The Wall was a high black ribbon that wound around the lip of the plague zone. It looked slippery, glassy. I found a broken pole, leaned it against the top, and climbed. Jessica was right; it was not difficult to cross.

The clinic beyond was a low stucco building. It had about it an air of general neglect. The windows were greasy, the paint peeling, the concrete walk filthy. There had been a sign over the door, its presence attested to by an oblong of faintly lighter paint. In its place were two holes with splintered edges. Forty-five caliber, at least. Someone had taken a disliking to Dr. Lorimar.

Inside the building was an elderly secretary who looked at me apprehensively.

"May I help you?"

"I'd like to see Dr. Lorimar," I said.

"The doctor never sees patients before noon." She fingered a string of pearls as though it were a rosary.

"He'll see me," I said. "It's kind of an emergency."

"I'm sorry." Her mouth snapped shut angrily. "Those

are his express orders. Never before noon." She glanced at a clock. It said a few minutes after nine.

I reached into a pocket, removed the piece of paper Jessica had given me. "Give this to him," I said. "He'll see me then."

She still hesitated, one hand on the pearls, one hand nervously holding the note.

"What's the matter?"

She looked embarrassed. "Dr. Lorimar never takes patients before noon because . . . well, because he is unable to."

A light burst.

"Is he drunk?"

The old lady nodded.

"Where is he?" I snatched the note back and headed for the rear of the clinic.

"Wait a minute . . . you can't . . ." she began. By the time she'd managed to tell me I couldn't, I already had.

Dr. Lorimar was a rumpled little man in his mid-fifties with a web-work of cheek veins and a fringe of russet hair. He was sleeping it off on a makeshift day bed.

He wasn't really that out of it, or maybe he just held it well. After a shower and two cups of coffee he functioned sufficiently to bark at his secretary for some breakfast. Then he looked at me with sad brown eyes that didn't evade. I liked him immediately.

"Well, what's this all about?" he asked. He sipped at the second cup of coffee and paused to light a cigarette.

I proffered the note. He read it, examined it, put it in his pocket. He looked suddenly older, warier, as though a fire had burned through him.

"What's your name?" he asked.

"Gil Warren."

He stared, then very quietly got up and closed the door. Then he sat down again and raised his eyebrows in amazement. Finally he said, "I read the papers. According to them, you're dead."

I grinned at him and shrugged. "I might as well be. They gave me a mind-rub." I told him then of my abandonment in the slime pits and my subsequent interment in Jessica's cellar. He heard me out, finished his cigarette, lit another.

"How much do you really know about Jessica Dos Santos?" he asked after a while. He gave me a measured look.

"She was one of Fannon's experiments," I said. "Other than that, not much. She has that Medusa field I told you about—that's working on me as I sit here."

Lorimar didn't seem much affected. He finished his cigarette and crushed the butt in an ashtray. The secretary came in then with eggs and dry toast and Lorimar dived in. He located another coffee cup and poured it full for me and waited until the woman had gone before speaking again.

"Does she have anyone else trapped in that field?"

"A man named Tuttle. A couple of zombies named Tidman and Dickson."

Lorimar nodded and took a bite of toast.

"Tidman," he said after a moment, "was head of security for Fannon Enterprises. People tended to disappear when they crossed him. When Jessica escaped he was sent after her."

"He found her," I said dryly. "Only it was a case of the fly finding the spider."

Lorimar went on as though he hadn't heard. "When Tidman did not return, Fannon sent in Dickson—a soldier, an ex-commando. His orders were to take her out any way he could."

I lit a cigarette and sipped Lorimar's coffee. I could see preconceived notions flying away on the wings of a zephyr wind. A lot of things suddenly made sense that hadn't before.

"The last one to go after her was Tuttle," Lorimar was saying. "Fannon handpicked him to do the job. He'd done a lot of work over in Europe, had about twenty hits."

I was silent. It occurred to me suddenly that Jessica Dos Santos was quite a . . . well, not a lady, exactly, but quite something nonetheless. I would tell her that when I got back. I finished the coffee, set it aside.

"Where do you fit in?" I asked. I noticed that despite the sun, the room was becoming darker. Odd.

"Oh, nowhere much," Lorimar said in a suddenly deep voice. "I worked on the Medusa Project; I knew Jessica. After Fannon sent in Tuttle I found a corpse that looked near enough like her and signed a death certificate. I burned the body. I figured if she could survive Fannon's three assassins she deserved a chance to be left alone."

"Fannon bought that?" I asked. Things were starting to drift a little. Visual disorientation. I wondered why I didn't care.

"I had witnesses," Lorimar said in sepulchral tones. "Pictures. If he wasn't convinced he never said so."

"But he had you blacklisted." It was a statement, not a question.

Lorimar nodded. "I was a loose end. Fannon never liked loose ends."

Suddenly something was happening, blotting out my senses, turning the world to rubber. I thought—*it was in the coffee* . . . I heard Lorimar as from a great distance and felt myself falling. And then I felt nothing at all.

Consciousness did not come back all at once. There was a mosaic of light, a susurrus of sound. Then my vision slowly cleared. Lorimar was standing over me, his face pale in the moonlight. I felt terrible. Sick.

Moonlight?

"Take it easy," Lorimar said. He bent down close to me, broke an ampoule of acrid-smelling stuff. It took away the cobwebs, left me sitting up, coughing. It was then I noticed the straitjacket.

I mumbled, "What gives?"

"Just a little precaution," Lorimar told me, smiling. Then he closed the curtains and turned on the lights. "Gangs come around the clinic sometimes," he said apologetically. "No reason to give them a target."

I remembered the holes in the sign. Someone hadn't liked his bedside manner, and judging from experience, I couldn't entirely blame them.

Something sledged my gut then, and I emptied my breakfast on his carpet. He'd been expecting it; he cleaned it up, gave me a drink of water.

I said, "I feel lousy."

"I know. Give it time." He lit a cigarette, held it so I could inhale. "You're breaking away from a strong ca-thexis field," he said softly. "It's going to take most of the night. It's going to be a little difficult."

I heaved again, leaned back against the bed, glared at him. "Where is Jessica?"

He shook his head. "You would know that, perhaps, better than I." He looked at me sharply. "You know she took quite a chance, bringing you here. Devilishly risky."

I tried to talk, and couldn't. A rivet gun had begun hammering boiler plate beneath the roof of my scalp. Lorimar said something I didn't hear. I flopped around on the bed like a sackful of wolverines, tasted blood, saw darkness and light in strobelike discontinuity.

Lorimar had said it would be going on like this for the remainder of the night. And, oh yes, it was going to be a little *difficult*. I hoped to God he was wrong.

He wasn't, though.

"Here, you'd better get something to eat." Lorimar held up my head and spooned something hot into me.

He left the straitjacket on, just in case. I noticed it was daylight outside.

"I need a cigarette," I said.

He lit one and held it for me. He was a conscientious caretaker, I had to give him that. He had probably been a fine surgeon. His eyes were red-rimmed from lack of sleep and he needed a shave. But I didn't smell any liquor on his breath and his hands were reasonably steady.

I said, "Thanks."

He just nodded, past subtle pleasantries. He gave me more food, a shot that made the room glow cosily, and then stretched me out again. I closed my eyes.

This time I slept ten hours straight.

When I woke up he took the straitjacket off. He had used the time to get some sleep himself; his eyes had gone back to being just sad, not red and sad. He hadn't shaved, though, and the stubble around his jaw and cheeks looked like a rusty wire brush.

"Well, how do you feel?" he asked.

"Much better," I said. "Does this thing recur? Will I suddenly fall into a foaming fit like . . . ?"

He laughed and broke the train of thought. "No. Barring further association with a Medusa, you're cured."

"You mean there are more like Jessica?"

"A couple. Fannon was intrigued with the concept; he kept the project alive after Jessica disappeared. None of them are as strong as she is, of course." He raised his eyebrows. "How about some coffee and something solid to eat?"

I was suddenly famished. He went to the door, opened it a bit, and I heard a rumbling of conversation. In a moment he came back.

"Nellie is putting something together," he said. "In the meantime, let's talk about you."

I said, "Hold on a minute. Let me get something

straight. Jessica deliberately saw to it that I came here, knowing that you'd break the cathect?"

He stared at me a long time, then said quietly, "That's what she *hoped* would happen."

"So now she's alone again—with Tuttle and the other two."

"They're bound to her," Lorimar said. "A cathect that deep can't be broken without severe trauma." He paused. "It was nearly too late for you. She cut it very fine."

I thought of Jessica, suddenly saw electrons spinning about a neutron. That's what Tidman, Dickson, and Tuttle were, I thought. Electrons. And I had been a fourth, only I'd just been kicked out of the electron shell. I wondered idly if I had raised or lowered the valence.

Nellie came in just then with a tray of food and I said, my mind still wandering, "She's quite a woman."

Lorimar made the differentiation. He took the tray, smiled at the old lady, answered, "Yes, she is." He put the tray on the bed straddling my legs and then helped himself to a heavily buttered biscuit.

When Nellie had gone out shaking her head, I said, "Jessica said something about beating the mind-rub, getting my memory back. *Is* there a way?"

"There's been some research into it," Lorimar said unenthusiastically. "None very promising. Mind-rubbing derived from electroshock techniques. It leaves pretty much a blank slate."

"That's a pity," I said darkly. "I seem to have had such an interesting past."

He managed a tiny grin. "What I can do is *rebuild* your memory—using school records, first-person reports, the memories other people have *of* you."

But I said, "My memory is not gone, doctor. There just aren't any faces, any names, any *people*."

"Interesting," Lorimar said. "And impossible. A mind-rub is not selective."

"Which leaves an inescapable conclusion," I said in the ensuing silence. "Whatever was done to me—wasn't done with a mind-rub."

He nodded, looking thoughtful.

I spent the rest of the day sleeping fitfully, waking in cold sweats. Lorimar had left half a pack of cigarettes on the bedside table, and I went through them, feeling the restlessness inside of me. At nine o'clock Lorimar showed up with dinner.

"Hungry?"

"Enough. Not too."

"That's good. Because all I could find was roast beef and potato salad." He put the food on a lap tray, set it in front of me.

"How do you feel?"

"I want to see Jessica," I said, picking at the food. "Just one more time."

He didn't look surprised. "Oh? Why?"

"I don't *know*, man! Just to *see* her." I ground my teeth together angrily.

"Okay."

"Okay?"

He sat down on the edge of the bed. "If you *do* see her again, you'll end up like Tidman and Dickson—a goddamn zombie. You want that?"

"That doesn't *have* to happen."

"Yes it does." He looked at me a trifle sadly.

Jesus! I took a mouthful of roast beef and thought about Jessica Dos Santos. *She* still *had strings on me*.

My recovery was slow. It took a week for the restlessness to end, another before I had whole days of autonomous thought. Lorimar was patient; I was not.

He did not protest when I said I wanted to see the

place where I had killed Avery Fannon. He did suggest, however, that I exercise common sense and put on some kind of disguise.

Gilliam Warren's face had been on every television screen and newsfax across the country; it would be instantly recognizable. He bought me a fake beard and light-tinted contact lenses. Putting them on brought on an attack of *deja vu*.

"No one's looking for you," Lorimar told me when I was ready to go. "For all intents and purposes you're a dead man. Keep it that way."

It was funny, I thought. Jessica Dos Santos had said the very same thing.

Chapter Twenty

I entered the museum through the main entrance, past the nine stone daughters of Mnemosyne, identified in iron: the Muses.

I stopped at Euterpe's foot. No one took notice. I mingled with the crowd, drifted. Fifteen minutes later I passed into the other wing and descended the great stone stairs.

I slowed where the wall curved away and showed signs of newly polished brick. It had happened here, a small contained explosion, a clap of dry thunder. A body had broken, stone and steel were splashed with red. *The king is dead—long live the king.* I grimaced and turned away. I felt no grief, no remorse. It was not guilt I lacked, but simple *references* for guilt.

My eyes lifted then, and I looked upon wonder. A centaur gazed sagely back, his great brassy head attentive, mobile. I moved closer, read the inscription beneath. Chiron. Lord of Surgeons.

Beyond the centaur was another wonder, a nude girl descending a staircase. *Alive. Motion stilled but held, like bated breath.* The I.D. plate said simply: *Cassie.*

* * *

"I have some questions for you," Lorimar said. He sank into the chair beside his desk, propped up a foot, looked at me with speculation.

"Go ahead," I said.

"What exactly do you remember? And I mean *exactly*."

I thought about it for a moment before replying. Then I said, "My left leg aches sometimes. When that occurs I imagine I see helicopters—lots of them—being blasted out of the sky." I paused and felt perspiration on my forehead. "I hear screams all around me, too, but no one is ever there. No people, no faces."

"Anything else?"

"There was a place where I always went swimming," I said, casting about. "I rescued somebody there, saved him/her from drowning." I paused, shaking my head. "I can remember the thrashing in the water—but no face. Goddamn it, Lorimar—*there is no face!*"

"You'd be surprised," Lorimar said with a faint shrug. "Most remembrances tend to be people-specific. Take away that orientation and the scene loses meaning— enough, even, to defy recall."

"So what happened to me?" I stared at him with something like anger.

"Somebody used a Zyman box on you," Lorimar told me. He lit his first cigarette of the evening and deposited the match in an already overloaded ashtray. He was dressed in a faded, uncreased suit, and he was still sober.

"From the look on your face that must not be fun," I said.

His lips made an upward twitch. "It's strictly experimental. The effect is like slicing away a person's life inch by bloody inch. There's a rumor the police have been using it in interrogation. Needless to say, it's an effective tool."

"Of torture."

He nodded.

I looked at him. "Is the damage permanent?"

He knocked off a half inch of ash and shrugged. "I don't know—apparently nobody's ever researched it. Consensus is that everything depends upon the skill of the man wielding the thing."

That conjured up pleasant thoughts, I mused sardonically. I said, "So I have to hope my headsman was an artist with the axe."

"Something like that," Lorimar agreed.

I lit a cigarette of my own, inhaled, blew out a fist of smoke. "When can we begin that research?" I asked. "I don't know if I'll like what you find, but it's one way to while away the evening." I gave him what might pass for a grin.

Lorimar shook his head vehemently. "I can't do it, Gil. I'd be as delicate as a hippo on a highwire. The sort of operation we're talking about requires someone with an intimate knowledge of Zyman box parameters—and a magician's touch to boot." His eyes flicked from the smoldering tip of his cigarette to where I sat facing him.

"You know anybody like that?" I asked.

He shrugged. "Four or five. But if I contact them, word will get around in a hurry. You won't be safe any longer."

Muscles jumped at the corners of his jaws.

"Something else?"

He nodded. "What if the one I ask is the one who did the original work on you?"

I said, "Ouch," and acknowledged his point. It would be nice to have someone working on me who had my best interests at heart. Like Lorimar, who'd even given up his booze.

I put out my cigarette and went to him.

"Let's take it slow," I said. "I'd prefer to get all the marbles back."

He grunted. "I'll work on it." His sad eyes looked sadder than ever.

*   *   *

I spent the next four days in the library synthesizing a past for myself. I had discovered it was next to impossible to recall accurately an event—place, time, occurrence—without reference to peopling. I invented wraith forms who came and sat and halfway filled the chinks.

Mr. Shakespeare, meet Peter Pan. I believe we all went to school together . . .

Hell!

So I had holes in my head . . . or at least in my mind.

Sometimes in the afternoons I went to the museum, always to the brazen centaur, the nude descending.

Thus it was the other woman spoke to me.

"I've seen you here before," she said. "I can tell—you're fascinated by Warmath's work."

I turned and took in a wealth of raven-wing hair, large candor-filled eyes. She was wearing a blue wraparound that did pleasant things to her figure.

"He has a gift," I said only, and left it hanging, open-ended.

She laughed. "Ye gods! Yes, I'd say he has a gift. I think he's magnificent!" She looked at the frozen figures, then at me. "Do you know him?"

"No."

"I do. He's going to be here next week."

I looked at her with more interest. "My name is Jack Michaels," I said. "I'm in research work. Dull stuff, mostly. Coming here makes the day seem more worthwhile."

She smiled. "I know what you mean. I'm Frances Willow. Hi."

We shook hands briefly, then examined the sculptures from the perspective of a stranger's eyes. I learned more than she did. We shared a cup of coffee in the museum's snack shop and she told me how she made her living. She was a dancer.

"Tap, toe, or ballroom?" I asked, a cup of coffee halfway to my lips.

"Saloon," she said, and grinned.

"I've narrowed it down to one man," Lorimar said. He leaned back in his chair and steepled his fingers. His sad eyes found mine and blinked.

"Who is he?"

"Old Lawrence Zyman himself. If he can be persuaded to take it on."

"There's doubt of that?"

Lorimar snorted. "The man's a virtual hermit. He comes out of seclusion maybe once or twice a year. He does outstanding work, though, and he's absolutely to be trusted. He would be shocked that someone had so misused his invention."

I said, "Maybe that's an angle you can use, then. Perhaps he'll feel he has a certain responsibility to make things right."

Lorimar shook his head. "You don't understand Lawrence Zyman. He's a law unto himself. An eccentric. You wouldn't get to him with anything as prosaic as that."

I waited, then, "So how *do* we get to him?"

Lorimar shrugged. "That's what I keep wondering. Give me a few days to think about it."

Summer sun, blistering heat. Something substantial in it in a way—a palpable reality.

I walked through sidewalk shimmer. Above me whirled the space platform known as Up-Top. I'd read about it—it and the Gods. I had killed two of them, it seemed, in some uncanny fashion.

Here I had done it. In this museum. I stood outside and looked at it, and then I entered.

For an hour I sat and felt the peace that comes from

merely existing in the presence of friends. I drew in
psychic strength from their massive auras.

Chiron.

Cassie.

Then, as I rose to go, I heard a voice hailing me.

"Jack!"

Smiling, I said, "Hello, Frances."

"There's someone here I want you to meet," Frances
Willow said. She presented a smallish man who had
gnarled forearms and laugh lines at the corners of his
eyes. She said, "Julius Warmath, Jack Michaels. Jack,
Julius."

I said, "Hello," and watched the man's face fall apart.

He recovered quickly enough. He flattened the planes
of his face, murmured a greeting, shook my hand.

But he had seen something, and it had shaken him.
He had seen it through the tint of my eyes and the
screen of the false beard. *Damn his artist's eyes!* For he
had those kind—the kind that strip away outer layers to
the bone.

I glanced quickly at Frances, but she had seen
nothing—it had happened very rapidly indeed.

"So you like *Centaur*," Warmath said.

"Yes."

"And *Cassie*."

"That, too."

"Ah." He gave a wicked little grin and looked at his
wrist, where there was a band of gold and carnelian. He
looked back, caught my eye.

"Would you join us for dinner, Mr. Michaels? It's
getting to be that time."

I said, "No, thank you. I have to be getting back." I
muttered a few words to Frances to cover myself and
made a hurried departure. I glanced back once, saw
Warmath staring after me, his round face expressionless.

I paused outside the museum to consider my next

move. I could not go back to the clinic—at least not immediately. When the artist notified the police the streets would not be safe.

Damn!

I went left, toward the river. I walked at a pace just short of a run, turning at the first crossing I came to, flowing with the crowd.

Farther on, where a collection of small shops broke up the block, I turned and cut through a small alley. Then I found a dive sufficiently dim and parked myself in a back booth with a view of the door. I ordered a bottle of beer from a sour-smelling slattern and settled back to think.

Mr. Shakespeare: *Hark! The pikemen on the heath bode ill, methinks.*

Gil Warren: *At the very least, William.*

Mr. Shakespeare: *S'ooth. Come hither, come hither, come hither:*

> *Here shall ye see*
> *No enemy*
> *But winter and rough weather.*

Gil Warren: *You've got it a teensy bit wrong, Bard.*

Mr. Pan: *He knows it. What you really need is a magic ring, friend Gil.*

Gil Warren: *What I need is my memory back. Faces to put in empty frames.*

Mr. Pan and Mr. Shakespeare: *Ah, you're as an unperfect actor on the stage . . .*

Gil Warren: *Shut up, all!"*

I could think of nothing better to do, so I did nothing. I drank my beer and ordered another. I gave it until dusk, then went out the back way into the alley. It was empty, the only obstruction a turned over garbage barrel.

I was almost at the entrance when the shadow appeared.

"Gil?"

I recognized the short muscular figure of Julius Warmath. He seemed to be alone, but there was no way to tell for sure. I stood perfectly still for almost a second, my weight poised on the balls of my feet. The alley ran back past the bar exit to the edge of the river. There would be boats there, perhaps an avenue of escape.

"You know me," I said. "That makes the advantage all yours."

"Don't run," Warmath hissed. "You don't have to. There's nobody with me."

I permitted myself to relax, ever so slightly. Warmath was strong, but I was certain I could defeat him in hand-to-hand combat.

He came forward perhaps half a dozen steps, and stopped, peering at me in the dusk.

"I wouldn't have risked following you," he said abruptly, "except that time is running out for us—*for all of us*. Will you take a moment, talk to me?"

He had dropped his arms to his sides, showing himself to be vulnerable. I hesitated for an instant, thought of *Chiron*, of *Cassie*. This man had created them. If he had just a tenth the character he'd given them . . .

I dropped my arms too, stood quietly.

"I'm listening," I said.

He stared at me, face creased with sudden lines. Clearly, he was puzzled.

"You don't know me?"

"No."

"I read in the papers that you'd been caught, killed . . ."

"As far as the Triumvirate knows, I am dead," I said. "I want it to stay that way."

"But my god! I *can* tell Cassie, can't I?" He stared at me for a second or two and then smote the side of his head. "You don't remember Cassie, either, do you?"

"No. Unless you mean the sculpture."

His grin was spontaneous, unfeigned. He murmured,

"Boy, have *you* got a surprise in store. The sculpture's rubbish compared to the real thing."

He examined me anew. "Where you staying, Gil?"

"A friend's place. I don't know if it's safe to take you there."

He shrugged. "There's no place in this world that's really safe, my boy. Not any longer. But I suggest we *do* get out of this alley. In another hour or two the local cutthroats will have their way with us."

"Let's go, then," I said. "I'm just going to have to take a chance on you."

Chapter Twenty-One

"You're Julius Warmath—the artist," Dr. Lorimar remarked increduously. "I recognize you!" His arms jerked into motion and his eyebrows shot up.

"I am," Warmath acknowledged with a courtly old-world bow. He sat down on Lorimar's daybed, his knobby forearms close to his sides. He looked at the doctor closely. "Gil has told me you've been helping him. I want to add my thanks to his."

"You knew Gil pretty well, did you? The *old* Gil?"

"We've spent some time together," the little artist admitted with a grunt. "Mostly, though, I come in second fiddle to a girl we are both fond of."

"You're rivals?"

Warmath laughed. "Twenty years ago, maybe. Not now, though."

Lorimar nodded as if it all made sense, put on a pot of coffee, washed three cups, placed them before us.

"Cream and sugar?"

"Black," Warmath said, and when he had tasted it, sighed appreciatively. I sipped my own, Lorimar his, and we all three gauged this particular new development.

There was silence while all this was going on, not

oppressive. The sculptor topped off his cup with fresh coffee and I lit a cigarette. Outside the wan moon cast a faint opalescent net about the city. I heard dogs baying, and the quiet whisper of a breeze stirring along the Black Wall. It was a lovely night for horror stories.

When Warmath first talked to me in the alley I had—at first—been unwilling to believe him. But his words were spoken with a simple force . . . *and he had known me!*

At some point you make a decision—to accept, to trust. I looked into Warmath's eyes, saw that which lay at the heart of Chiron. I let out a breath I hadn't known I was holding.

I believed.

On the way to Lorimar's clinic he put his hand on my shoulder, gave it a squeeze.

"Don't remember *any*thing?"

"Oh, sure, things," I said. "But no faces . . . no people. Sorry—I don't remember you."

"What about that sinker you teleported? You still do that?"

I said, "What do you mean—teleport?"

"Humph." He shook his head sadly. Then he perked up a bit and grumbled in a bass voice, "Cassie's missed you, you nitwit. I'm going to do my best to fetch you back to her."

Lorimar put his coffee cup down, crossed his legs. "If *you* recognized Gil, then others will, too. We'll have to work on that disguise. You never can tell when one of the Gods is looking."

Warmath looked grim. "Someday there'll be a reckoning—a trial, like Nuremburg. Until then we just have to keep going." He looked at me speculatively. "And maybe—just maybe—Gil is the man to bring them to justice."

"What do you mean?" Lorimar asked, staring at the other.

"Because Gil *himself* is a God," Warmath replied calmly. "Earthbound and hunted, but a God nonetheless."

Lorimar's eyes went round as a tarsier's.

"He has a Talent," the little artist went on. "A damned interesting one. If he could get Up-Top, he might be able to use it against the others."

Lorimar ran his fingers through his bush of hair. "Gil is that much stronger than the Triumvirate?" He looked at me in fresh appraisal.

The sculptor shook his head. "He's certainly stronger, but that's beside the point. It's not a matter of degree. It is a question of *kind*."

I studied the liquid in my cup for a moment, then set it down on the table. "I don't like hiding, much," I said abruptly. "If I can get my memory back—and my Talent, whatever *that* is—I'll work against the Gods."

Warmath gave me his puckish grin.

Lorimar pursed his lips, looked wise.

Chapter Twenty-Two

Julius Warmath was a man of decision. He was a shaker and a doer. He whisked us north toward the mountains, his rented electric at top rev. Above us the sky paled, grew fingers of salmon hue.

"What if the Gods find us?" Lorimar wanted to know.

"Their visits are not without warning," Warmath said, a trace of a smile on his face. He held up his left arm. Gold and carnelian gleamed in the soft light. "Telltales. There's a demonstrable change in the ion count just before they make their appearance." He chuckled. "Or nonappearance, as the case may be." He patted the telltales. "I've got these all over the castle. Gives me an easy two or three seconds to look innocent."

"They visit you often?"

"In the beginning they did; lately, not. Guess they're too busy building that shrine out in Utah." He glanced over at the physician. "What did you say that inventor's name was?"

"Lawrence Zyman."

"You think he can undo the damage to Gil's memory?"

"If anyone can," Lorimar said, nodding.

The little artist punched numbers into the radio-phone and was rewarded by a deep baritone voice coming from the speaker.

"Warmath residence. May I help you?"

"This is the boss, Aldis. Get hold of Frannie at her hotel. We need to persuade a Lawrence Zyman, inventor, to visit us in the near future. Like tomorrow. If she needs help, tell her to holler." Parenthetically, he added, "He's in the book."

"Yes, sir. Anything else?"

"I'm bringing two guests; they'll be staying a while. We'll need to dust off the pigeon roost for them." Warmath hung up and directed his attention to the road. I noticed that he was grinning slightly. A busy man is a happy man.

Another hour brought us to the foothills of the mountains. It grew hotter as we climbed, and the view became scenic. Presently we were among huge stands of pine.

"Here we are," Warmath said sometime later. He swung the car off onto a winding lane, stopped in front of an iron portcullis that opened when he rang through on an intercom. After a moment a fairy castle came into view, all turrets and high stone walls.

"You were here once," Warmath told me. "Remember?"

I shrugged. "Something. Like the tail ends of dreams."

Inside, we followed paneled hallways to a large common room hung with heraldic tapestries.

There was a girl there, tall, gray-eyed, slender. I recognized her immediately. *Cassie*. Or not—merely the mortal embodiment of nude descending. *Merely*—!

She said, "Hello," and looked into my eyes.

"Hello."

"You don't know me . . . ?"

"No," I said. "Sorry. No."

"He's misplaced your face," Warmath told her lightly.

"We're going to help him look for it." He bestowed a kiss on her cheek with clear relish.

"Aldis!"

A gray form materialized.

"Yes, sir?"

"Is the pigeon roost ready?"

"Yes, sir. I've stocked it for a three-week stay."

The little sculptor nodded. "That should be sufficient."

The pigeon roost was a five-room fallout shelter beneath the castle's wine cellar. The floor was stone and cold, the walls lined with books of all kinds. The ceilings were high, vaulted, not unlike a cathedral.

Lawrence Zyman arrived the following afternoon, never feeling the wounds of kidnap. Frances Willow, her sylph-like form poured into a dress of pure demonred, purred against him like a well-fed tabby.

Grinning wickedly, Warmath greeted the inventor and made introductions. Then he kissed Frances Willow on the nose.

He said, "You ought to be arrested, woman. Or at the very least made to wear a warning tag."

Lawrence Zyman was about seventy, extraordinarily light-skinned, with blue eyes set deeply in their sockets. Despite appearances, he looked like a man who knew his own mind. If he had succumbed to enticement, it had been as much from curiosity as anything else.

He said, "I have heard of this castle of yours, Warmath. Shangri-La North, it's been called. I had to see it for myself." He grinned, and his voice was soft, but there was a current of steel underlying it.

The sculptor grinned his showman's grin.

"By all means," he said. "Shall we start in the library and then tour the upstairs? There are some original Louis XIV pieces you may be interested in."

That evening, after dinner, we sat in the artist's study and talked of Zyman boxes and the enmity of gods.

"I had heard they were misusing the Zyman Effect," Zyman said. "But then it is a tool, and nothing more. Any instrument may be misused."

"True. There is no accusation against you." Warmath crossed to a comfortably appointed bar and selected a bottle of brandy. As he opened it he looked back at the inventor. "It is said, though, that you are a master practitioner as well as a theoretician. *Can* you repair damage done by a Zyman box?"

"I've done so in a few cases," Zyman returned. He accepted a glass from the artist and sipped at the liquid.

"Gil—"

I took off my false beard and popped out the tinted lenses. I looked at Lawrence Zyman, held his gaze.

"Will you accept me as a client?"

He recognized me, of course, and his eyes flickered. "I thought you were dead."

"A fiction I would prefer to maintain."

"I see." He glanced around, eyes not missing much. "And what if I choose not to take you as a client?"

"Then we will see to it that you arrive home safely."

He thought about it for ten seconds, then nodded. "Very well. Come to my laboratory in two days' time."

"We would like to do it here," Warmath said gently.

"Oh? But my equipment—"

"We have sufficient equipment," the sculptor said. "I've located a Zyman box and had it delivered here. And Dr. Lorimar will be a most able assistant."

"Very well. When shall we begin?"

"Why not right now?" I suggested.

"Now?" He shrugged. "Indeed, why not?"

And we began.

I felt the band about my head, heard the spitting sound that came from it. Sweat I tasted, and bile.

"It hurts," I said.

"Umm." Zyman took a hypo, filled it, injected the contents into my arm. I stared upwards and began counting. At twelve the vaulted ceiling seemed to flush with light. At fifteen the light shimmered, became the universe.

A single sound, a single form. A forest of snakes, their sibilant whispers filling eternity. They rotated in a backward fashion, became a face with saucer-sized eyes.

"Jessica!"

"Medusa to you, chum. I see you've made it this far."

"Yes."

"Do you realize how few people have the chance to start everything all over again—new memories, new life? Forget this. Go back to being Jack."

"The Gods won't let me, Medusa."

She gave me a basilisk stare. "That so? Humph." But the head rotated again, forward this time, and she said: "Well, go on then, take one."

"Take one?"

"Snake, dummy. Pick one."

They were all hissing, turning themselves into angry knots. I put my hand on a small one, pulled.

It bit, and I yelled out. There was pain, and an inward flowing current that jerked my head back.

"Pick another."

"It hurts."

"Of course it hurts. You thought this was going to be easy?"

I put my hand on a pit viper, felt it writhe against my skin. I pulled, was bitten. Came the current, flaring along my synapses like runaway ball lightning.

When I picked myself up, I said, "Look, what is this accomplishing?"

"Don't you know?"

"No."

"Dummy. You remember a girl named Cynthia you

used to take hiking in the woods? You were about twelve then, and you thought she had the biggest pair . . ."

I said, "Sure! She used to like—" and stopped, my mouth hanging open.

"That's right," the Medusa said. "You remember a face." She grinned gleefully and lowered her head. Snakes bit at me. I selected the closest one, pulled.

When I'd picked myself up for the dozenth time, I detected a softening of the light. And there were shadows, where no shadows had been before. The pains within my head were fierce, as though someone were hammering in a spike that had barbs on it.

Then Medusa abruptly vanished. The universe gulped and swallowed me up.

I opened my eyes and beheld again the vaulted ceiling of the pigeon roost.

"Well?" Said through tight-clenched teeth: Zyman and Lorimar.

"It's slow," I said. "But it's coming back. I have my childhood now, and my youth."

Zyman nodded and removed the band from my head.

"And it hurts," I said. "Almost more than I can bear."

"That's because I have to amplify what little remains of each identity," Zyman said. "It will get worse, not better. Do you want to stop?"

I looked at him, at Lorimar.

"No."

"Very well. But we're going to have to go slowly. There's lots of psychic scar tissue—there may be trauma."

"How long will it take?"

He shrugged. "Two days, three. It all depends on how much you can tolerate. We're doing in reverse what was done to you earlier, you know; you're reliving that torture."

I knew, and God, the snakes did bite!

*   *   *

I ate and slept and brooded, and finally it was time
again. I lay on the pallet, looking up and counting.
Light flooded my vision. The ceiling went away.

"Back again?"

I looked upon Medusa, saw her tresses of coral and
cobra and copperhead. She saw me wince, and her
smile was white and wide.

"Yes," I said. "I'm back."

And her head lowered and the air was full of snakes. . . .

It took three days and left me near death. I was glad
then of Lorimar and his sad, caring eyes.

I slept, and this time there were no dreams.

"You're going to suffer side effects," Zyman told me
some time later. I was sitting up, smoking a cigarette.

"What kind of side effects?"

"Depression. Nausea. Bouts of pain." He shrugged.
"The man who did this to you had only one thing in
mind—to make you suffer. He didn't intend that you
should ever come out of it."

"His name was Sandone," I said, and my mind's eyes
conjured up a round face with thick-lensed glasses,
glinting blue irises, thin, controlled lips.

Catherine came in then and I took her hand almost
shyly. We talked for half an hour, until Lorimar entered with his needle.

Depression. Nausea. Bouts of pain. Those things that
Zyman had said would happen, did. I awakened in the
night, head splitting, stomach churning.

Goddamn Sandone!

I turned on a light, rose to my feet.

"Gil?" Lorimar's form materialized from another room.

"Make it stop! Goddamn it, give me something!" I
clutched my head with both hands, sweat pouring freely
down my cheeks.

Almost gently, he led me back to bed. "I can't, Gil.

Anything stronger right now would cause irreparable damage."

I gripped the pillow in a stranglehold and convulsed half a dozen times.

Lorimar massaged the back of my neck.

"I remember every damn thing he did to me," I croaked. "The *shit!*"

"You *must* remember," Lorimar returned, his thumbs sinking into muscles. "That's the only cure."

I cursed into the pillow until, little by little, the pain subsided. After a time sleep came again.

Chapter Twenty-Three

"Can you walk?"

"I can *try*." I leaned against Lorimar and half raised myself from the bed. Five days and nights I had fought my demon, walking closer to the edge than I ever had before. Only my hatred kept me sane. That, and Lorimar's unbending resolve that I survive.

I walked, and slept, and the days passed. Somehow, I came to accept the penalty of remembering.

I stood beneath one of the ornate chandeliers of the pigeon roost, holding a glass of Scotch in one hand and flipping through a book of poems. I stopped when I came to one by Louise Guiney.

> I hear in my heart, I hear in
> its ominous pulses,
> All day, on the road, the hoofs of invisible horses,
> All night, from their stalls, the importunate pawing
> and neighing . . .

I heard a sound, turned.

"I'm glad you're feeling better," Warmath said. "But didn't Dr. Lorimar tell you to stay in bed?"

"I was getting antsy," I said. "I felt the need for a

little exercise." I removed a crumpled pack of cigarettes from my pocket, lit one. "Has Zyman gone?"

"Yes."

"Can he be trusted not to talk?"

"He has no use for Gods. If he's anything, he's an anarchist. I don't think we'll have to worry about him."

I agreed with that. Zyman had struck me as a man who does things because he *chooses* to do them, and for no other reason.

Warmath looked at me. "I've been meaning to ask. Can you still do your disappearing trick?"

I didn't know, but now was as good a time as any to find out. I shook a cigarette out of its pack, tore off the filter, held the little cylinder of cellulose between my fingers. I went into set.

The filter did not vanish. Instead, I found myself choking back a groan. Pain beat like hot lava against my temples.

"You okay?"

I gritted my teeth. "Fine."

"You don't *look* fine." He gave me a worried look. "I'll get Lorimar."

Presently, I found myself back in bed, wires running from my body to half a dozen machines. Lorimar took a day and half, ran battery after battery of EEG scans while I tried to teleport a flyspeck-sized piece of metal.

"There's something seriously wrong here," he mused, looking at a paper printout.

"What?"

"It looks as if some brain cells have been damaged."

"Oh?"

"Not many—just enough to make the readings anomalous."

"You mean when I use the sets—try to teleport something?"

He put the printout down, shook his head. "I'm afraid so. Somebody really worked you over."

"Sandone."

He nodded. "You won't be using those sets you talked about. The moment you try it, feedback takes place— *destructive* feedback—like a pair of microphones that've been brought too close together. That's what causes the pain." He worried his lower lip and peered at me. "And if you persist, you'll end up either dead or insane."

"There's nothing you can do?"

"You can't just rearrange brain cells, Gil."

"No, but—"

"Forget it."

"Then Sandone's won," I said numbly.

He looked at me sadly. "I suppose he has."

Catherine brought me dinner, and we shared it, sitting at one of the huge library tables that filled the center of the pigeon roost.

She said, "I've been staying here since . . . what happened at the museum. Julius thought it would be safer."

"Have the Gods bothered you much?"

She studied my face. "When you disappeared, they were here constantly. Sometimes they just watched us, invisible as ghosts. Damned eerie, if you want to know."

"So Warmath developed the telltale that early."

"Yes."

"The underground would give a lot to have something like that," I told her.

"Julius has already given it to a local group." Catherine took a bite of salad, put the fork down. "You know, I hoped you would call at first—and then that you wouldn't—they'd be waiting for that."

"I thought about it," I said. "Many times."

There was silence for three or four seconds, and then she said: "Dr. Lorimar says you've lost your Talent."

"That's right."

"Does that mean you're no danger to Sandone anymore? Can you be just Gil Warren again?" She raised her hand, touched my cheek, smiled.

"Not really. Sandone thinks I'm dead. It's going to have to stay that way."

We finished the meal, and she picked up the tray.

"I'll be back later," she said with her old impish grin, "to tuck you in."

I fell asleep immediately after Catherine left for the second time. I dreamed of Sandone, and of mandalas. There is a peculiar chemistry in dreams, and in that inward place I was still Sisyphus, my wits as sharp as ever, my strength undiminished.

Toward morning I awakened, startled by a thought. Sandone had won, if that meant I could no longer teleport objects. But what of those things already pushed up Everest's slopes? Retrieving *them* had become almost a reflex, one that required little energy.

It doesn't take much effort to fall off a mountain.

I sat up in bed, turned on a light. Sitting there in a lotus position, I reviewed my inventory.

It was not particularly large, but it *was* varied. I settled for a Roosevelt dime, pictured it in my mind, drew upon my dwindled resources.

It took time, and effort, but in the end the coin rested passively in the palm of my hand.

In the morning I told Warmath and Lorimar, demonstrated by making a duplicate coin appear in the sculptor's cupped hands.

He grinned at me, relief written all over his face. "Maybe we *do* have a chance. How many items do you have 'up there'?"

"Not very many. Two hundred or so."

The little artist grinned again. "It will have to be enough. Now it remains to get you Up-Top—to the Babylon Gate."

"Easier said than done, I'm afraid."

He stroked his chin and gave me a look of cunning. "Let me worry about that. You get some rest."

"You know something I don't?"

He twitched his shoulders, looked pleased with himself.

"Of course I do."

The nausea was the worst thing, worse even than the depression and pain. It came on suddenly, leaving me weak, gasping. Lorimar had given me pills, but they only softened the edges, did nothing to stop the visceral heaving.

It would come and go, Zyman had said. Perhaps with time the effects would lessen. Perhaps.

Goddamn your eyes, Sandone!

It was about eight o'clock on the tenth day of my recovery when Warmath revealed his plan to take over Up-Top.

"Go to the shrine," he said. "It's not complete yet, but petitions are still being heard. Get an audience with whomever's in charge."

"Oh? Suitably disguised, I hope."

He nodded. "And suitably accompanied. We want to make certain you receive their full attention." Grinning like a Cheshire cat, he opened the door and made a grand bow. Showman to the last.

He made his point, though. It *was* likely we'd get their full attention.

Alicia Fannon walked into the room.

She had changed in the months since I'd seen her last. There was a grimness about her mouth, a haunted quality in her eyes. She seemed thinner, too, and more intense.

She stopped when she saw me. Her eyes did not hold hate, though I had killed her father and her lover. My brother.

She said, "I understand you want to go Up-Top."

"Yes."

"Then I will take you there."

"You know your uncle will oppose us." It was not a question.

She nodded briefly, selected a chair, sat. She was wearing slacks and a white blouse belted in green. She looked dangerous, and likely was. Her father had raised her to be independent, and that independence had been his undoing.

"Why do you want to do it?" I asked. "Is it because of what the Gods have become?"

"Partly that," she replied. She gave a tentative smile, dropped it. "I'm tired of running."

"And partly—?"

She shrugged. "This has gone on long enough. We don't need gods to hold our hands." The smile again. "Even when they're relatives."

Chapter Twenty-Four

It was warm outside the castle, the night air perfumed with the scent of mountain laurel and honeysuckle. The moon had grown, and stared down with a somber and sallow eye.

"Time to go," Alicia said.

"Yes." I opened the car door for her, closed it behind her.

A door opened, and light spilled on the ground in soft pools.

"I won't say good luck," Catherine said.

"No. Wait for me."

"Yes."

And I got into the car and drove.

We left the car, Warmath's rental, in the nearest town, and caught a train across the mountains. From there we went to an airport and booked passage to Salt Lake City. There was a longish wait before the flight, which gave us time for breakfast.

"I used to hate you," Alicia Fannon said. "I used to want you dead." She stirred her coffee moodily and stared out the window at the burgeoning day. There were a few faint clouds in the sky, high up, waiting to be shredded by the sun.

"Oh, why?"

"Because you gave me away to my father." She gave me a glance, looked away.

"I didn't know why you were running away," I said, and shrugged. "For that matter, I still don't."

She put her spoon aside and raised the cup to her lips. Her eyes, even through the dark glasses, were green and penetrating.

"There was a time," she murmured, putting down the cup, "when I loved my father. He was strong—the strongest man I knew. He was rich, and powerful, and people looked up to him."

"But something changed your mind."

She went on as though she had not heard. "Oh, there were some who said bad things about him, but then jealous people are . . . jealous, are they not? He gave me everything I wanted. Money, yachts—"

"He was a taker," I said, loud enough to stop her.

"What?"

"Avery Fannon thrived on power," I said brutally. "And he didn't care much how he got it. He was a textbook case—a living definition of a sociopath."

For an instant she froze, her hand tensed on the table top. Then she relaxed visibly, a tight little grin playing across her lips.

"You're not the first to say that. Mark said that, too."

"He did?"

She nodded. "Before he went Up-Top, we had some long conversations about Father." Her grin grew more forced. "Mostly detrimental to our relationship. Then, somehow, he seemed to change. He'd been working with Father on the Babylon Gate. He became almost protective."

"Oh?"

She picked up the spoon, looked at it, put it down

again. She smoothed her blonde wig, said, "That's when I began to get frightened. I stayed down here, away from him—and away from Mark, too."

Something clicked inside my head. I had a blurred image of Jessica Dos Santos, of her cadre of walking zombies.

"Son of a bitch!" I exclaimed. "Of course! He had a Medusa field!"

Alicia jerked her head back, looked at me with wide questioning eyes.

It was the only thing that made sense. Fannon's researches had paid off—he had controlled the telekines by using a variant of Jessica's cathexis field. Maybe he could even turn it on and off.

Alicia said something, but I did not hear. I was seeing Mark again, his body plummeting downward, reaching for Fannon even as he fell. *Like a moth caught in a flame* . . .

Alicia took my hand, stood up.

She said, "Come on. I think our plane is boarding."

The Shrine of the Gods was a truncated pyramid half a mile square. It had a starkness about it, a simplicity that bespoke a trained and articulate eye. Whose idea was it, I wondered. Heywood's? Morse's? Or perhaps Sandone himself had laid it out.

Beyond the great doors of redwood and steel was a hall that opened into a room the size of an airplane hangar. On one wall was a mutated innerscape of clinging moss and bright yellow flowers; on another, crossed staffs, symbol of the Chosen. Briefly, there had been three such staffs.

I stopped for a short time in a lavatory to check my disguise. I took in the rather prominent nose, the belligerent chin. I laughed at myself out of flat blue eyes.

Ah, Sisyphus, I thought. *Welcome back.*

When I rejoined Alicia I took my time and looked

over the room. It was filled with vacationers and tourists. Here and there were guides in the black livery of the Gods.

"Come on," I said. I followed one of them back to his office, a cubbyhole beneath a vast arcing stair.

"Who is in charge here?" I asked.

The guide glanced up. He was youngish, with just the beginnings of a moustache.

"Do you wish to make a petition?"

I smiled at him. "Yes, I think you could say that."

"Petitions are taken on the second floor. Just up those stairs."

"And who is in charge up there?"

"Colonel Partin. He'll see that your petition is entered properly."

We climbed. The second floor was rich in wall sculptures, holographs of myth and legend. Above us a mighty Titan stretched forth his arms: child of Uranus, get of Gaea. Then, on a gigantic wall screen, there were stars, and the rotating silvered form of the space platform. Up-Top. Home of the Gods.

We stopped at a long table flanked by two black-clad attendants.

I said, "I want to speak to Colonel Partin."

One of them pointed to a tall, heavyset man. I walked over to him, tapped him on the shoulder.

"Colonel?"

He turned and looked at me, then over my shoulder at Alicia.

"Yes?"

"We would like to talk to you—in private."

He looked annoyed. "I don't give private audiences. They'll take your petition at the desk."

"This is not an ordinary petition, Colonel. This concerns Fred Sandone and the space platform itself."

His eyes narrowed dangerously. He studied me for a moment, then switched his gaze to Alicia.

"What is this about?"

"Two minutes of your time, Colonel. That's all we want."

He stared at us while he thought about it. At last he came to a decision, nodded toward a bank of glass-paneled doors.

"Very well. Two minutes only. Follow me." He led the way into one of the offices and closed the door. He turned, then, and placed both hands on his hips.

"Well—make it good."

I said, "We want to go Up-Top, Colonel."

He was startled, and his hand was suddenly very near his coat pocket. He said, "That's impossible. No one goes Up-Top any longer—except the Gods."

I held both hands clear of my body. There was no need to get him upset.

I said, "Contact them. Situations change."

His hand was in his pocket now, and I said, "Alicia?"

She gave him a thousand-kilowatt smile and removed her wig and glasses.

"Don't tell me you don't recognize me, Colonel. That would be very disappointing."

He stared. I didn't blame him. The hand left the pocket, though, and he stood a little straighter.

"Miss Fannon . . . I . . . still can't contact the platform. I've been given strict orders."

Alicia sat down in a chair and put her feet up on the desk.

"We'll pass over the fact that I'm Avery Fannon's heir, Colonel, and that I *own* all of this. I'm only interested in talking to Uncle Fred at the moment. Do you think you can arrange that?"

"I . . . well . . ."

"It will be my responsibility, of course. You won't get into trouble." She favored him with another smile, this one conspiratorial.

Before he had time to think about it, I snapped, "Well, Colonel—what's it to be?"

He started to say something, thought better of it. He closed his mouth and nodded.

"Please wait here. I'll arrange a contact." He turned around smartly, opened the door, and was gone.

We looked at each other. I hummed a tune from "South Pacific." Step one.

"That was almost *too* easy," Alicia said suddenly. She looked worried.

I shook my head, dug out a cigarette, lit it. "You don't know your own charisma, lady. If your friend the colonel had gotten any more rigid, you could have used him for a nail."

There was a pause, and then abruptly, she grinned. Another thousand-kilowatt effort, this one for me.

"What—" I began, and then stopped. The gold carbuncle I was wearing on my left index finger suddenly gave me a twinge. I looked casually around, saw nothing. Sometimes, though, it's what you *don't* see. I began a discourse on the aesthetics of throwing together a pile of marble like the Shrine. I didn't have to lie; so far, I'd been impressed.

The door, which had been open a few inches, closed with a bang. There was a sudden swirl of dust on the desk top. A head formed, in vague outline. It was missing a good deal of its substance; the eyes were simply hollowed areas beneath a suggestion of a brow, the glasses little more than an idea. I remembered another simulacrum, that of Fannon himself, with Mark controlling it from the Gate. If this shadow-skull was the best they could come up with, they were weaker than I thought.

The thing opened its mouth. "Hello, Alicia," said Fred Sandone.

"Hello, Uncle."

The head swiveled a little.

"Who is your friend?"

Alicia smiled. "My husband. His name is Jack Michaels, uncle. He's the one who persuaded me to come here."

"Oh." Sandone's rasping voice grew still. I was aware of quiet scrutiny, of a licking presence that flowed toward me, sat for too long a time on my shoulder. The carbuncle telltale was going crazy on my finger.

I lit another cigarette, thought coldly of memories that flickered away like fireflies. I thought of a harmless little man—a clown—named Sam Portner.

Bide your time, Sisyphus . . .

The presence flowed away and the simulacrum spoke again.

"Welcome, Jack Michaels. You are to be congratulated. Many men have tried to take this woman to the altar."

"Thanks." I smiled and nodded and tried to look properly connubial. The simulacrum swiveled back to Alicia.

"You choose an awkward method of making your announcement, my dear. There are problems that must be worked out; we have little time for rejoicing, I'm afraid."

Alicia made a dismissive gesture with her hand. "I know you're busy, Uncle Fred. I won't keep you any longer. I just wanted you to meet Jack—and know that we won't be hiding out any longer."

"Tell him about the underground," I said curtly.

"Oh no, Jack—" She looked at me ingenuously, shook her head.

I brought my eyebrows down, stared at her fiercely. "They've threatened her, Mr. Sandone. But she won't tell me who they are or what they intend to do."

The simulacrum opened and closed its mouth. "You should listen to your husband," it said soothingly. "Who are these people?"

"Jack is exaggerating things, Uncle Fred. They wouldn't really *do* anything." She gave me a black look and lit a cigarette of her own.

Part of the simulacrum dissolved, reasserted itself. It said, "On the contrary, my dear. I'm sure they would, if the opportunity presented itself. They could use you to threaten Up-Top."

Alicia shook her head. "No. They wouldn't."

"I'm afraid we can't take that chance. Be prepared to come up in the shuttle tomorrow morning. See that she is ready, Jack." Sandone's rasping voice was firm, allowing no room for debate.

"Yes, sir."

The Sandone-thing abruptly fell apart, the dust falling loosely on the desk top. The telltale still twinged, however, and I played it out for our unseen observer.

I said, "You see? Your uncle thinks you're in danger."

She gave me an icy stare and crushed out her cigarette.

"When are you going to learn to keep your mouth shut? I don't want to go Up-Top. I want to stay down here."

"But *I* want you to go up—where you'll be safe."

We had a spat, after which we held hands and made up. Finally, much later than I might have thought, the telltale gave us the all-clear.

Chapter Twenty-Five

It was eerie, riding a shuttle that stole empty into the morning sky. Our voices were hushed, lest they echo in the seating compartment. We watched the Earth recede in colors of pearl and frost and aquamarine, and much later, when I looked through the scanner ports, I saw the spinning sparkling toy where dwelt the gods.

It was about that time that the nausea hit. I stumbled into the lavatory, threw up into the "positive flow" toilet. It was all too much a remembrance of mortality. As I sank back into my seat, I licked my lips for moisture. I tasted blood instead, where I had bitten through the flesh.

I missed the docking, but I was able to move all right when the airlocks unsealed. Gripping my stomach, I followed Alicia through into the Platform. We were met by a uniformed man wearing the emblem of crossed staffs. I recognized him immediately—the ubiquitous Colonel Phillips.

He smiled, looked at me closely, frowned, then indicated a corridor to our left.

We were given five well-appointed rooms on one of the outer corridors. Scanner ports showed us a sable field of stars, then, as the Platform swung around, the pocked empty face of the moon.

"Mr. Sandone will see you at lunch," Phillips said. He paused at the door and looked back. "It's good to have you back aboard, Miss Fannon." His face turned ruddy. "Excuse me—Mrs. Michaels."

Alicia laughed. "That's all right. I'm not used to it either."

When we were alone, I asked, "Do you know everyone up here?"

She looked at me, shrugged. "Some of them. I had the run of the place while the Gate was being built. I was underfoot a lot." As she spoke she upended her purse onto the bed, then selected three items from the pile—a lipstick, a hairclip, a gold cigarette case. She broke the case open, folded it back upon itself, then screwed the lipstick onto the revealed threads. She telescoped the lipstick tube out to its full length, added the clip to the undercarriage, where it made a fully functional trigger mechanism.

"Julius does exquisite work," she said, hefting the small weapon. "It's accurate to thirty yards."

"Let's hope you won't have to use it."

She made a move toward the door, then stopped and turned. She gave me a puzzled look. "That man stared at you a long time. Does he know you?"

"His name is Phillips. He was a field man for Sandone. Something about me might have tugged at his memory, but that's as far as it'll go. I'm dead, remember?"

"Uh huh." She opened the door, peered down the corridor. "But just in case, I think we should move *now*."

"It suits me." I stepped around her, looked both ways. The corridor was clear. To my left were the inner rings—and the Babylon Gate—to my right, the crew's quarters and the platform bridge.

"Let's go," I said, and we both turned right.

With each step we took I could feel the coldness taking me, turning me into a walking statue.

We encountered no one until we were halfway to the bridge. Then a man wearing a mechanic's belt came out of a utility room and saw us. He paused, regarded us with raised eyebrows.

I said curtly, "Where's Phillips? Or the captain?"

"Colonel Phillips is probably off duty now. The captain is on the bridge. Who're you?"

"More important," I said curtly, "is who *this* is. Don't you recognize Alicia Fannon?"

"Uh, yes sir." He stood straighter, squared his shoulders.

"What's your name?" Alicia asked in softer tones. She put a hand on his shoulder, bestowed upon him one of her charismatic smiles.

"Johnson, ma'am."

"We'd like to see the captain. Would you take us there?"

He hesitated only a moment before nodding and pointing left along the corridor. We followed him through several locks, emerged finally in an open space flanked with monitors and computer mainframes.

"That elevator will take you right up to the bridge," Johnson said. He indicated a steel enclosure just ahead.

I said, "Thanks," and strode past him toward the elevator. When I had taken two steps I stopped and turned. I said, "Oh, by the way, what's the captain's name?"

He appeared startled, but said, "Wilson," and then his eyes narrowed. Before he could think it through Alicia stepped up behind him and slapped an ampoule to the back of his neck. He looked confused, as if a bee had stung him. He took a step, then went glassy-eyed and began to fall. I caught him before he could hurt

himself. Then I half-dragged, half-carried his inert form
to an out-of-the-way spot behind a storage bin.

Stepping into the elevator, I glanced at Alicia. Her
expression was one of composure, of subdued excitement, her carriage that of a soldier. She had, I thought,
more than a little of her father in her.

"Ready?" she said, her voice harsh. She gripped the
little weapon lightly, holding it with elbow bent so that
the barrel was directed straight up.

I grinned at her. "Ready."

The elevator stopped and we disembarked.

The bridge was that in name only. It was simply a
nerve center monitoring the platform's functions. The
control room was located above it, and that was where
true authority was vested.

There were four people on the bridge, one of them
wearing the blue tabs of a captain. He interrupted a
discussion with one of his subordinates when we entered, blinked twice, and then opened his mouth to
bawl a command. Abruptly, however, he sneezed, and
continued sneezing until Alicia placed the business end
of the gun beneath one ear.

"Okay, Gil—that's enough."

I looked at the subordinate. His face was set and a
little pale. He stood very quietly, eyes flickering from
me to Alicia.

"What do you want?" the captain finally managed.
His face was red, his breathing still mangled by the
quarter ounce of cayenne pepper I'd materialized in
front of his nose.

I ignored the captain, switched my gaze to the two
remaining crewmen. One was halfway out of a chair,
looking undecided about completing the action. The
other man, a lieutenant by the two blue pips he wore,
had headed toward the control room door.

"Stop that man!" I snapped at the captain. "If you
don't, I will!"

The captain's glance followed my pointing arm. Still strangling, he called out: "Squires, get the hell over here!"

The lieutenant had his hand on the door, and I thought it maybe fifty-fifty that he'd take his chances. He thought better of it, however, and turned slowly our way.

"How many are in the control room?" Alicia asked her charge. I watched his eyes as he digested events and tried to think of a way out. That he recognized Alicia could not be doubted; he seemed totally stunned by her actions. I, of course, was the unknown, and it was on me that his eyes dwelt longest.

He didn't answer her questions, but I didn't really expect he would. We herded all four of them to the other end of the bridge, and Alicia put them under with an ampoule apiece.

I went first into the control room, circling to my right so that there would be a wall at my back.

There were four more crewmen there, all of them sitting at consoles. We repeated the maneuver, and presently there were eight laid out like cordwood in the bridge.

"Time to go hunting," I said lightly. "Lock the door and don't let anyone in."

Alicia studied me and nodded. Then she smiled a little. "You're a fool, Gil. They're telekines, and you're outnumbered."

I didn't answer. Instead, I went through the control room door and closed it behind me. I could hear steel bars fall into place as Alicia dogged the locks.

I walked toward the inner rings. Toward the Babylon Gate.

Somewhere I'd read that gravity in the inner rings was kept at three-quarters Earth normal. I took note of the change as I got closer to my destination.

"Gil?" An intercom on the corridor wall whispered my name.

"What?"

"I've downloaded information on the crew," Alicia reported. "There's a total of seventeen. We've accounted for nine."

"I hope none of them get in my way," I said, and shrugged. I continued walking.

"You're crazy," Alicia said to my back.

I came to a branching corridor, turned to my right, and hesitated. Avery Fannon's office was just ahead. Chances were that Sandone would be occupying it now.

Surprise was my best ally. I opened the door and stepped through, then turned and locked it behind me.

Sandone wasn't in the room, but two other people were. One was facing toward me, his hands full of computer reels. The other was seated, engrossed in a series of computer-generated graphs.

I smiled at the first man, stepped close to him, put my hand on his shoulder. He grimaced as the ampoule's stinger discharged its contents.

He said, "Who are you?" in a puzzled voice. Then his face registered shock and he began to collapse. Computer reels crashed loudly on the floor.

The second man looked up but did not rise. He watched events with narrowed eyes, and then said, "He asked a good question—who the hell *are* you?"

"The name's Warren," I said. "And Chesbro. And Michaels, and maybe a few others you don't know about. Hello, Heywood."

We stared at each other. The telekine was a trifle shorter than I, and lighter by maybe twenty pounds. His large head was capped by fuzzy blonde hair, dominated by wide-set blue eyes.

Was he the murderer, I wondered, or was Morse?

Heywood abruptly stood, smiled at me with calculated humor. "You know what you're dealing with, Warren?"

"I think so."

He shook his head. "I really doubt it. If you did, you'd have stayed away from me." And then his grin grew fixed.

He didn't move, but something else did. A letter opener spun off a desk and flew toward me. I batted it out of the air, summoned a rain of pea-sized stones. When he ducked beneath them I made him a present of two ounces of finely ground cayenne. He sneezed, took a step back—and the letter opener stirred where it lay, did a mad jig across the floor, its point aimed inelegantly at my crotch.

I averted my eyes, materialized half an ounce of polylux, and heard him curse as it exploded.

Then I stepped close and hit him as hard as I could where the mandible breaks off from the jaw to form the zygomatic arch. He fell, his head slamming against the edge of the desk.

I checked his pulse, found it strong and even. Just to be sure he would stay put, I used an ampoule.

The telescreen on the desk lit up. Alicia looked out at me.

"They found Johnson. That means that Sandone has been warned. They'll be waiting for you, Gil."

"What about you? You okay?"

She nodded. "They'll try to break in, but that will take some time." She gave me a conspiratorial grin. "And I can delay them too, since I control platform functions."

I said, "Keep me posted," and headed toward the door.

Chapter Twenty-Six

Morse was waiting for me in the corridor leading to the Babylon Gate. I got a sense of his size as I moved closer, and felt sweat break out on my forehead. *Jesus!* He was little short of a mountain.

He watched me, smiling through his beard, his eyes soft, almost dreamy.

For Morse, I knew suddenly, killing people was probably a simple joy—and maybe the closest he'd ever come to a religious experience. There was no question any longer who the murderer was.

He studied me as I advanced, then grumbled in a monotone, "We thought you were dead."

"You and Heywood are sloppy workmen."

"Not me," he said, head shaking. "Sandone wanted you alive—at first. Now you've made him afraid—and that's funny."

"But you're not afraid," I remarked. "You're enjoying the whole thing."

"Right you are." He grinned, held out his arms almost affectionately. "Come to me, Gil. I don't promise to be quick. Not with you."

"You're too goddamn eager," I told him. I searched

237

above Everest for something appropriate, found it, pulled. Morse was hit by a blizzard of acid droplets.

It affected him, but he managed to shunt most of them away. Then he snarled and his grin went away. I felt something clutch my heart, give a brief beat of pain. An invisible hand grabbed the back of my neck, jerked me forward.

"Now . . . now . . . now," he growled in his throat. His immense hands reached out for me.

I tried the cayenne, but it seemed to have little effect. His fingers found my shoulders, and his mouth opened a little in delight. Opened, as it happened, just far enough.

I blew his head off with my last micro-grenade.

I said, "Where's Sandone? He's not near the Gate."

"Somebody blew out all the circuits leading down to ring one," the intercom murmured in Alicia's calm tones. "There's still power for lights, but it's blinded all the cameras there."

"It gives a direction," I said. "How are things up at the Bridge?"

"Getting interesting."

"Hold them off for another hour. That should be long enough."

"Watch your back, Gil. I won't be able to help you down there."

"Thanks," I said. "Watch your own."

I got a chuckle as the intercom clicked off.

Not being used to low gravity, I took my time about moving down the rings into the hub. Sandone was still Sandone, and in his own way, he was probably more dangerous than Morse.

The hub was an open space filled with lashed-down boxes and equipment. There was a null-gravity laboratory at one end, a recreation area at the other. I glanced around. Lots of places for a man to hide.

"Gil?"

I turned, one hand on a stanchion. I saw a dim figure in the shadows thrown off by a gantry.

"Hello, Fred." I moved slowly toward him.

The shadow moved, resolved itself.

"Phillips!"

He smiled a little, and off to my left there was a harsh booming explosion. Something spun me around and made my right leg go limp. I continued my spin until I struck the wall, then caught myself by grabbing one of the structure supports. A voice inside me was screaming, *Decoy . . . !*

Phillips made as though to retreat into the shadows. I gave him a halo of steel pellets to speed him on his way. Then I turned and considered the short-legged man who was drifting slowly toward me.

He was armed with a rifle with heat-seeking bullets; I recognized the make and model. As he got closer I could see the hatred in his eyes, almost feel the raw weight of that emotion.

"Bastard . . . why won't you die?" he queried to the empty air. He stopped his forward motion, tipped up the rifle, stared at me over the barrel.

My leg was useless. It was a good thing there was no gravity. I watched Fred Sandone as his finger tightened on the trigger. My hand found the hole in my leg and tried to hold back the blood.

"Gonna make *sure* of you this time," he grated heavily. "*Damn* sure!"

I ground out, "It would be a mistake, Fred. Just give up—godhood doesn't become you."

His finger tightened and the gun went off—off being in several pieces and in all directions. A bullet-sized piece of lead lodged in the barrel tends to do that to a firearm.

The recoil had pushed him back against the gantry. He rubbed his numb arm and stared at me.

"*Damn* you!" He reached into his belt, pulled out a pistol.

His second mistake. I put an ounce or so of water inside his cranial sinuses. Then I pushed myself over and took his toys away from him.

Just before she fitted the Gate over my head, Alicia leaned forward and kissed me.

She said, "That's for not killing him."

"It was close."

She nodded. "Yes."

Then the hood came down and the power whined up, ratcheting like a runaway crosscut, and I forgot about breathing.

The Earth hung below me, touched with blue, delicate, a jewel lost in the immensity of space. My eyes seemed ten feet around, and I could brush the heavens with my fingertips.

God! No wonder they claimed brotherhood with legend.

I descended Earthward, let it turn beneath me, plummeted. I halted fifteen feet above a shining stretch of sand. Overhead gulls wheeled, around me the air blew in hard gusts, kissing the wave tops, sending salty foam onto the beach. I drifted lower, went inland. I looked upon an old Jesuit mission, saw a band of Clockers preparing a fire.

I watched, and I exulted, as though my bloodstream already pulsed with pi-dalinol. I rose then, and sped eastward, over water and over land. I looked upon the great house on the point and searched for Skeeter John.

The cottages were empty, the secret room filled with rubble and dirt, the pipeline clogged.

Up again, and west, where the Black Wall lay like a circle of inky glass. I sped through empty streets, down into a hidden cellerway. It was dark, and the rain pounded a rough tattoo on the broken steps. I entered, sought light beyond an arch.

"Jessica," I said, but no words came. I was not a telekine, could not vibrate air. I cursed. *To be a god, and have only eyes . . .*

I rose into the night sky then, and past the swelling moon. Out I went, toward Mars and then beyond. Jupiter loomed, filled the sky, fell away.

Out there, in the trackless black, I rested, and found a kind of peace.

Some time later I came back to the platform. I removed the helmet that connected me to the Babylon Gate and looked up at Alicia.

"How long was I gone?"

"About an hour."

"That's interesting. This thing distorts the time sense. I could have sworn I had been gone five or six." I looked at her. "Did you get hold of Warmath?"

She nodded. "He's ready to come up. Catherine, too."

"Good. Let's get the shuttle ready."

It took several hours for the shuttle to drop down to Earth and return with its passengers. While that was going on Alicia and I grabbed a sandwich in the galley.

With Sandone and his men under wraps, it was pointed out to the technicians and other personnel that Alicia Fannon was merely claiming her inheritance. They thought it over for less than a minute before they voted to continue working for Fannon Enterprises.

We met Warmath and Catherine in Avery Fannon's old office, where the walls were rubbed walnut and the carpet piling came up around my ankles.

"You've been hurt!" Catherine looked at the bloody bandage on my leg. Her eyes met mine for a moment, and she came forward and took my hand.

"It will be all right," I told her. "It looks a lot gorier than it is."

Chapter Twenty-Seven

In my apartment in Pittsburgh, things were pretty much as I had left them. The Night Watch was still in its shrine, the french windows still looked out on a city caught between centuries. A time would come, I suppose, when the smokestacks stopped their pollution of the air. That time, however, was not yet.

I read a book I'd been promising to myself. I slept and ate, and watched television. And most of a week wound itself into a ball like string. My bad leg healed while that was happening.

The telephone rang every day, but I ignored it, and after a while whoever it was stopped trying to get me.

On the fifth day someone held their thumb on the doorchime until I unwired the thing and dropped the magnet into the trash.

I had a lot to think out—a need for solace, and quiet.

When I woke up on the eighth day I saw someone had pushed an envelope under the door. It lay there until dusk, until something resembling curiosity made me reach down and pick it up.

In neat print, it said, *Gil, glad to see you're back. If*

you want an accounting, I'll be at that bar off Turner Road. You remember the one. —Baldwin Fowler.

I thought about it for an hour, then I showered and put on slacks and a sweater. I strolled leisurely down the street, aware as if for the first time of the wonderful smells of the city, the soft breezes of late summer.

Fowler was waiting in the last booth, a wine glass in front of him. When he saw me he rose and took my hand.

"I ordered Neufchateau. They didn't have it, worse luck."

"A good house red will do," I said. "How have you been, Baldwin?"

"Fine, thanks." He seated himself, gave the order, peered at me over steepled hands. "*You* don't look so good, though. You're much too thin."

"I just need a steak," I told him. And I ordered one rare with mushrooms and onions.

"We were worried," he said next. "But Mr. Warmath said just to leave you alone—that you needed time to lick your wounds."

"God bless the Warmaths of the world."

He paused, took a sip of his drink, set it back down. Features drawn a bit, he said, "You'll pardon me if I say you look—different, somehow."

"Different? How?"

He shook his head. "I don't know. Older, maybe." He stopped, went on, "Like you know something the rest of us don't."

"That's true enough." When the wine came I sipped it slowly. "You mentioned an accounting," I said. "Would that be on my trust?"

"Yes." He smiled for the first time and draped his arm over the back of the booth. "I've managed to nearly double it. The research I did on Colebarth showed the shipping line was ripe for a takeover. I waited, and then invested at what I thought was the most propitious moment."

"Am I rich?"

"Considerably richer than most people in this town."

"Good." I smiled at him. "Got a half-dollar?"

He looked at me wonderingly, but dug a composition coin out of his pocket and passed it to me.

I said, "Thanks, Baldwin. Stay on the job. Right now I've got to call someone."

Catherine answered the phone on the third ring. I stared at her, at those unblinking gray eyes, and took a deep breath. "I'm back. There's a cabin up in the mountains—below Warmath's castle. Can I pick you up in an hour?"

She didn't say anything, but she didn't have to.

Autumn. Outside the cabin window leaves stirred, floated down like large brown flakes. I watched them fall through the twilight, settling softly.

There was movement down by the lake, a gleam of suntanned skin. Catherine came into view, saw me, waved. She carried a casting rod in one hand.

"There was a kingfisher down there," she said when she entered. "He was a real clown—and you missed it." She gave me a grin and a kiss.

"Did you catch anything for dinner, or do we starve?" I asked. I grinned back, came away from the window.

She hefted a wicker creel. "Trout. Two. And I think there's some wine left. That sound okay to you?"

"That sounds just fine," I said.

We ate, and afterwards took the bottle of wine and walked (I limped) up to the knoll that overlooked the lake. Warmath's castle was just visible through a break in the trees. We lay in a circle of grass and watched the shadows turn to flint and India ink. We drank the wine and made love. And I felt her tears on my chest.

"You're different, Gil. Changed . . . I don't know

. . . *some*how." She shrugged helplessly and drew her arms around me again.

After a time I lit a cigarette. And thought again about the Gate Up-Top. Who could use it and *not* be changed?

I turned as a fish flopped in the water. Ripples spread in silvery waves beneath us, reflecting starlight, radiating outward in long pulses.

"I think there's some wine left," Catherine said.

We drank it and made love again, there on the grass.

And in private moments I knew that Sisyphus was not truly dead . . . but only sleeping.

Announcing one hell of a shared universe!

OF COURSE IT'S A FANTASY . . . ISN'T IT?

Alexander the Great teams up with Julius Caesar and Achilles to refight the Trojan War—with Machiavelli as their intelligence officer and Cleopatra in charge of R&R . . . Yuri Andropov learns to Love the Bomb with the aid of The Blond Bombshell (she is the Devil's *very* private secretary) . . . Che Guevara Ups the Revolution with the help of Isaac Newton, Hemingway, and Confucius . . . And no less a bard than Homer records their adventures for posterity: of *course* it's a fantasy. It has to be, if you don't believe in Hell.

ALL YOU REALLY NEED IS FAITH . . .

But award-winning authors Gregory Benford, C. J. Cherryh, Janet Morris, and David Drake, co-creators of this multi-volume epic, insist that *Heroes in Hell* ® is something more. They say that all you really need is Faith, that if you accept the single postulate that Hell exists, your imagination will soar, taking you to a realm more magical and strangely satisfying than you would have believed possible.

COME TO HELL . . .

. . . where the battle of Good and Evil goes on apace in the most biased possible venue. There's no rougher, tougher place in the Known Universe of Discourse, and you *wouldn't* want to live there, but . . .

IT'S BRIGHT . . . FRESH . . . LIBERATING . . . AS HELL!

Co-created by some of the finest, most imaginative

talents writing today, *Heroes in Hell* ® offers a milieu more exciting than anything in American fiction since *A Connecticut Yankee in King Arthur's Court*. As bright and fresh a vision as any conceived by Borges, it's as accessible—and American—as apple pie.

EVERYONE WHO WAS ANYONE DOES IT

In fact, Janet Morris's Hell is so liberating to the imaginations of the authors involved that nearly a dozen major talents have vowed to join her for at least eight subsequent excursions to the Underworld, where—even as you read this—everyone who was anyone is meeting to hatch new plots, conquer new empires, and test the very limits of creation.

YOU'VE HEARD ABOUT IT—NOW GO THERE!

Join the finest writers, scientists, statesmen, strategists, and villains of history in Morris's Hell. The first volume, co-created by Janet Morris with C. J. Cherryh, Gregory Benford, and David Drake, will be on sale in March as the mass-market lead from Baen Books, and in April Baen will publish in hardcover the first *Heroes in Hell* spin-off novel, *The Gates of Hell*, by C. J. Cherryh and Janet Morris. We can promise you one Hell of a good time.

FOR A DOSE OF THAT OLD-TIME RELIGION (TO A MODERN BEAT), READ—

GRANT CALLIN

"Grant Callin's universe is a fascinating one; I look forward to seeing more of it."—*Larry Niven*

"Grant Callin is a pro who knows space like the back of his hand. With this book he shares the excitement of exploring our newest, greatest frontier." —*David Brin*

"A very distant descendant of *Treasure Island*, but the 'treasure map' and the action it stirs up are thoroughly different from anything Robert Louis Stevenson could have imagined."—*Analog*

JANUARY 1986 • 65546-9 • 288 pp. • $2.95